PROJECT Z

A ZOMBIE ATE MY HOMEWORK!

D0051355

Copyright © 2019 by Tommy Greenwald
Illustrations by Dave Bardin, © 2019 Scholastic Inc.

All rights reserved. Published by Scholastic Inc., *Publishers since 1920*.
SCHOLASTIC and associated logos are trademarks and/or registered
trademarks of Scholastic Inc.

ISBN 978-1-338-30592-0

10 9 8 7 6 5 4 3 2 1   19 20 21 22 23

Printed in the U.S.A. 40

First printing, May 2019

Book design by Yaffa Jaskoll

Photos © Shutterstock: page i and thoughout:
burst (KannaA), page v and thoughout:
emojis (Ink Drop), page xii and throughout:
stamp (ducu59us), page 21: paper (schab), page 225
and throughout: paper (Forgem).

PROJECT Z

A ZOMBIE ATE MY HOMEWORK!

TOMMY GREENWALD

Math
* 4 + 4 = 8
* 10 + 12 = 22
* 18 + 8 = 26
* 9 + 19 = 28

SCHOLASTIC INC.

Dedicated to

JONNY "PAL" GREENWALD

Father. Doctor. Mensch.

On TV shows today, there are lots of different reasons why zombies are created. Sometimes storytellers explain that people are turned into zombies through breathing in dangerous chemicals or through catching mysterious diseases. To make these TV zombies seem extra scary, storytellers often have zombies being violent and even eating human flesh.

—Marguerite Johnson, July 2017

Don't believe everything you think . . .

—Anna Chancellor
(and a lot of other people, probably)

THE UNITED STATES GOVERNMENT
PROCLAMATION 358249-A
JULY 19, 2024
<u>TOP SECURITY CLEARANCE ONLY</u>

WHEREBY OUR NATION CONTINUES IN ITS SEARCH FOR COMMON GROUND;

WHEREBY THESE UNITED STATES HAVE NOT FELT TRULY UNITED FOR DECADES;

WHEREBY THE FEDERAL GOVERNMENT HAS TRIED TO BRING THE PEOPLE TOGETHER THROUGH MULTIPLE INIATIVES—BOTH CLASSIFIED AND PUBLIC—AND NOT SUCCEEDED;

WHEREBY IN ORDER TO BECOME ONE COMMON PEOPLE, IT IS SOMETIMES NECESSARY TO FIND ONE COMMON ADVERSARY;

WE HEREBY DECLARE AUTHORIZATION OF THE HUMAN REANIMATION PROGRAM,

HEREAFTER KNOWN AS PROJECT Z,

IN WHICH SUBJECTS WILL BE DEVELOPED ACCORDING TO STANDARDS OF PROTOCOL LAID OUT BY EXECUTIVE ORDER 127, WHICH WILL INCLUDE BUT NOT BE LIMITED TO THE FOLLOWING CHARACTERISTICS:

HIGH IQ AND VOCABULARY
LIMITED SHORT-TERM MEMORY, NO LONG-TERM MEMORY
NO NEED FOR SLEEP
DIET OF JELLY BEANS AND WATER
AGGRESSION TOWARD HUMANS
FEAR OF LARGE ANIMALS
TRADITIONAL/EXPECTED PHYSICAL TRAITS, I.E., PALE SKIN, LIMITED MUSCLE MASS, LOW BODY FAT

THE UNITED STATES GOVERNMENT

PROCLAMATION 358249-A

JULY 19, 2024

TOP SECURITY CLEARANCE ONLY

EACH SUBJECT WILL BE MARKED WITH A RED STREAK ACROSS THE PUPILS OF THE EYES.

EACH SUBJECT WILL SECRETE A MALODOROUS LIQUID WHEN EXERTED OR STRESSED.

EACH SUBJECT WILL BE ABLE TO IMPART TEMPORARY PARALYSIS IN HUMANS THROUGH USE OF A NERVE-PINCHING TECHNIQUE KNOWN AS "THE ZOMBIE ZING"; IN TURN, EACH SUBJECT CAN THEMSELF BE TEMPORARILY PARALYZED THROUGH A THOROUGH DOUSING OF SALT KNOWN AS "THE SALT MELT."

IN ORDER FOR THE SUBJECTS TO FULLY REFLECT HUMAN SOCIETY, THERE WILL BE A SMALL SUBSAMPLE OF REANIMATED JUVENILES.

THIS PROGRAM WILL COMMENCE UNDER THE AUSPICES AND DIRECTION OF J. K. LABS, INCORPORATED. THE LAB WILL OPERATE IN COMPLETE TOP SECRECY AND ANONYMITY FOR THE PROTECTION OF ITS WORKERS.

THE UNITED STATES GOVERNMENT
PROCLAMATION 358249-A
JULY 19, 2024
<u>TOP SECURITY CLEARANCE ONLY</u>

PROGRESS AND PROCESS WILL BE DISSEMINATED ON A **NEED-TO-KNOW BASIS** ONLY.

ANY EXTERNAL DISPERSAL OF INFORMATION ABOUT THIS PROGRAM WILL BE CONSIDERED A TREASONOUS ACT.

TARGET DATE OF EXECUTION WILL BE JULY 1, 2028.

AND FINALLY—UPON IMPLEMENTATION OF THE PROGRAM, THE SUBJECTS WILL BECOME KNOWN BY THEIR PUBLIC NAME: ZOMBIES.

SIGNED ON THIS DATE,

Carter Shotwell

CARTER SHOTWELL
EXECUTIVE DIRECTOR
UNITED STATES SECURITY AGENCY

February 25, 2027
GT 278
PROJECT Z
THE OUTER BRANCH
ARIZONA

ATTENTION ALL UNITS: There was a breach at GT 278 today, circa 04:28 hours. An electric fence malfunctioned when a small animal, most likely a badger or a possum, gnawed through the wiring.

This is the first reported incident of a security breach at any government territory. Extra precautions have been put in place to make sure it is not repeated.

There were six confirmed escapees. Five have been accounted for, secured, and immediately returned to their pods.

One escapee is still at large. Description: small in stature, typical pale complexion, standard issue clothing, and orange identification tag.

Please be aware: He is a juvenile.

HORACE BRANTLEY
Regional Commander, National Martial Services

PROLOGUE

Have you ever seen a zombie run?

It's not pretty.

First of all, we're not the most coordinated species in the world, if you know what I mean. Our legs don't work very well. They're rubbery and elastic, and it kind of feels like trying to run in glue.

Also, we're not in very good shape. We have a lousy diet and almost never exercise.

But the main problem is, running is not a zombie activity. Running is a *human* activity. And we stink at human activities. Humans are bigger than us, and stronger than us, and believe it or not? *Meaner* than us.

So the bottom line is, we're not very good at running. Which is why, on that day when I found myself running for my life, I was pretty sure it wasn't going to end well.

My memories from that day are a blur. I remember being out in the yard for Morning Routine, and then there was a lot of noise and commotion, and I was pulled through a hole in the fence. I remember crawling, with dirt, and mud, and grass getting in my eyes. I remember jumping into a river and the water being very cold. I remember hearing the voices of the others and then human voices behind us. I remember trying to yell. I remember the humans catching up to us. I remember confusion and fear. I remember a man with a reddish-gray beard, chasing me with a big bag of salt in his hand.

And the last thing I remember is that all of a sudden, from one second to the next, I was falling, falling, falling, into a deep, dark hole. And then my head hit something hard, and I closed my eyes, and all the noise around me got softer and softer until it disappeared altogether.

And then everything went dark.

RESCUE

I opened my eyes, which is something I almost never do, because I almost never close them in the first place.

I looked around, but it was too dark to really see anything.

I had no idea where I was or what had happened to me.

So I closed my eyes again, just to see what it felt like.

It felt strange.

After a few more minutes, I opened my eyes again. The sun had started coming up in the sky, and it was light enough for me to see that I was laying in a deep ditch in the middle of nowhere. My head felt like a popped balloon, and my ears were full of dirt.

It didn't look like any place I'd ever been before.

But that's probably because I'd never been anywhere.

I tried to figure out what to do next, and all I could come

up with was: *Get up.* I remembered I had been running from something, so as soon as I climbed out of the ditch, I started running again—badly, of course.

And as I waited for someone to inevitably catch me and bring me back to my pod, I started thinking.

I thought about the fact that I was alone. I thought about the fact that I didn't know where I was or what I should do. And

I guess I was thinking so much, I didn't notice that I'd run out into the middle of the road and was about to get run over by a yellow pickup truck heading straight for me.

HOOOOOONNNNKKK!!!!

I dove out of the way just in time. The truck screeched to a halt, spraying gravel from the road into my face. I think a few pieces even got in my mouth.

They didn't taste very good.

A human man and a human woman got out of the truck. I could tell they were real humans by their coloring. The man had a brown mustache, and the woman was wearing a blue dress. The man held the woman's hand. That must have meant they were attached to each other in some way. Or perhaps they were scared. Or both.

They leaned over me.

"There you are," said the man.

"We've been looking for you," said the woman.

Words started ringing in my ears:

Humans are the enemy. Humans will hurt you.

I didn't know where these words came from. But I heard them again:

If you see a human, attack. Humans are the enemy. Humans will hurt you. If you see a human, attack.

I remembered these words from somewhere. They were orders. They were orders I was supposed to follow.

But I didn't.

I couldn't.

"Are there others?" the man asked the woman. "There were supposed to be others."

She shook her head. "I can't be sure."

So they knew who I was.

I was too afraid to move. *They're taking me back*, I thought. And then I thought, *I don't want to go back.*

"Are you hurt?" said the man. "You have a big bruise on your head, like you've taken a real fall. But you're okay?"

I nodded.

"You're so pale," said the man, looking me up and down. "And so skinny."

"I think you may be making him nervous, Bill," the woman said, looking at the man.

"Oh dear," said the man named Bill. "I'm so sorry. We're here to help you. You need to know that."

I stood up, took a deep non-breath, and tried to be

brave. It wasn't easy. People scare me. Way more than I scare them, I bet.

The man squatted down and looked into my eyes, then looked up at the woman. "Yup, there it is, honey. The red streak across the pupils. Just like you said." He smiled and shook his head. "Well, we sure are glad to have found you, young man."

The woman touched my orange ID tag lightly with her fingers. "Norbus Clacknozzle, is it? I think I remember you. Well, Norbus, my name's Jenny, and this is my husband, Bill."

The man called Bill stuck out his hand. I looked at it.

If a human acts friendly, Do not believe them. They are just trying to lure you in before attacking.

"You're supposed to shake," he said to me. He turned and shook Jenny's hand. "Like this, you see?"

I slowly brought my hand up, and Bill grabbed it with his. It was the first human hand I'd ever felt. It was softer than I'd imagined. And warm. Really warm.

"Nice to meet you," said Bill.

The woman called Jenny held out her hand, and I shook it. "My goodness, we need to get you a blanket," she said.

Bill chuckled. "I'm not so sure a blanket is going to warm him up, dear. Don't forget, he's a zombie."

So *that's* what I was.

"Do you remember where you come from?" Bill asked me. "Do you remember home?"

"The poor thing has no memory," Jenny said. "And no home."

I wasn't sure what they were talking about, but at least I knew why I felt so alone. Because I *was* alone.

I got into their truck, and Bill placed a long strap across my chest and buckled it.

"How old are you, young fella?" he asked. "Do you folks even have an age?"

I stared at him, partly because I was still too scared to speak and partly because I had no idea.

Jenny shook her head. "They don't officially have ages, Bill. He's a juvenile, that's what we call them."

Bill looked back at me while he started the truck. "You've got nothing to be afraid of, son," he said. "Not anymore."

As we drove away, a wave of confusion and exhaustion washed over me, but also a new feeling I'd never felt before. At first I didn't recognize what it was. Then I slowly figured it out.

It was hope.

MEETING LESTER

Jenny and Bill lived in a small house, but it was the biggest house I'd ever been in, because I'd never been in a house before.

"Hop on out," Bill said, after we pulled into their long dirt driveway. He opened the door of the truck. "It's okay. We don't bite."

"Interesting choice of words," Jenny said, and they both laughed softly.

I stayed in the car. Jenny leaned in through the open window. "Oh, don't be shy, Norbus. Is that how you pronounce it? NOR-bus?"

I nodded.

"Well, Norbus, I've got some cookies in the cupboard with your name on them," Bill said, clapping his hands together. "Chop, chop."

I didn't know what *chop, chop* meant, but it sounded scary. Bill saw the expression on my face and laughed. "It means hustle up," he said. They had a small yard that was fenced in. I could hear a dog barking, but fortunately it sounded very far away. Other than that, it was really quiet. There didn't seem to be another house around for miles.

"We like our peace and quiet," Bill said, as if he were reading my mind. "Nobody bothers us, and we don't bother anyone else."

"The idea of you bothering anyone seems both preposterous and implausible," I said.

They stared at me.

Those were the first words I'd spoken to them.

"Well, well," said Bill. "It's nice to hear your voice. But what's with the five-dollar words?"

I shrugged.

"Are you tired?" he asked.

"They don't sleep, Bill, you know that," said Jenny.

"But I bet they still get tired," Bill said, and he was right about that.

Jenny went upstairs, and I sat with Bill in the kitchen. Neither one of us said anything for a while. "How about a shower?" he asked finally.

I'd never taken a shower, but I wasn't about to tell him that. But I did have to tell him one thing. "I am incapable of eating anything except jelly beans. Do you have any jelly beans?"

Bill frowned. "Jelly beans?"

"Any colors and flavors are fine."

He looked amazed. "Really? Jenny never said anything about that. So the whole . . . eating brains thing?"

"That is nothing more than rumor and innuendo," I said.

"'Rumor and innuendo,'" Bill repeated. "Where'd you go to elementary school, Harvard?" He started opening and closing kitchen cabinets. "I don't believe we have any jelly beans on hand, but I'd be happy to go grab some."

He smiled at me, and I was finally starting to relax just a tiny bit when I heard a blood-curdling scream. (Well, it definitely would have curdled *my* blood, if I'd had any.)

"YAOOOOOWHAA!!"

Three seconds later, a human boy about twice my size

came sprinting into the kitchen, holding a black helmet in his hands. He was wearing a big backpack, which was wide open and had papers spilling out the sides. Jenny was right behind him, and I saw her shake her head at Bill, which I think meant, *No, I haven't told him about our guest.*

"What do we got snack-wise?!" the boy said, way too loudly. "I'm STARVING!" He turned toward the big white refrigerator that was in the middle of the room, and that was when he first noticed me. "What the heck?"

He walked over, his nose twitching. "Who's this kid?" He bent down and peered at me like I was some sort of science experiment gone wrong—which, I suppose, I was. "Yikes, kid, have you ever even seen the sun?" Then he noticed my orange tag and looked up at Jenny and Bill.

"What's going on here?"

"Sit down, Lester," Bill said to the large boy. The large boy sat down. "This is Norbus," Bill continued, motioning toward me. "He's a zombie."

Lester shot out of his chair. "A WHAT?!"

"A zombie," Bill repeated. "He was reanimated as part of a secret government experiment. Several of them escaped. We think all the others were recaptured."

The boy's eyes went as wide as flying saucers. "There's no such thing as zombies!"

"Yes, there are," Bill said.

"How do you know that?" the boy sputtered.

Bill and Jenny looked at each other.

"We just do," Jenny said.

"You gotta be kidding me," Lester muttered. "An actual, real-live, brains-eating zombie?"

"Not quite live and not quite brains-eating," Jenny said. "But otherwise, yup."

"They're not what you think," Bill said. "He's actually very nice."

"Are you serious?" wailed Lester. "He could probably kill us just by looking at us if he wanted!"

"I have no predisposition to kill you," I said, because I thought it might help.

"You have no predispo-*what*?" Lester stared at me, then back at Bill and Jenny. "So what is that thing doing in our house? Sitting at our kitchen *table*?"

Bill sat down next to me and looked up at his son. "We would tell you more if we could. But we can't."

"You *can't*, or you *won't*?" Lester stomped over to the refrigerator, opened it, and stared inside without moving. He wrinkled his nose in disgust. "I mean, it's not that I'm scared of him or anything, but just *look* at him. Like . . . GROSS!"

"I will thank you not to talk to, or about, our guest that

way," Jenny told Lester sharply. "He is alone and scared. Please be courteous. Perhaps we should begin with some proper introductions." She waited until the large boy finally turned back around and looked at me. "Lester, I'd like you to meet our friend Norbus Clacknozzle," she said.

"He's not *my* friend," Lester mumbled, so softly I could barely hear it.

I looked at Jenny, hoping that she wouldn't say what she was about to say next. But she did.

"Norbus," she said, "I'd like you to meet Lester. He's fourteen years old. And he's our son."

THE dINNER TABLE

Humans eat dinner around a nice wooden table.

Zombies eat dinner in muddy pens surrounded by soldiers and scientists.

Your way is better.

😦 😎 😃

Jenny, Bill, and Lester were all eating some kind of non-human meat, and it seemed like they were enjoying it very much. Lester was also drinking glass after glass of milk. I was staring down at a bowl full of jelly beans that Bill had been nice enough to buy for me. There must have been about a thousand jelly beans in the bowl.

So far I'd eaten three.

"So your last name is Kinder?" I asked.

They nodded. "Yep," said Bill. "And we try to live up to the name as best we can, don't we, Lester?"

Lester snorted, and a little bit of milk squirted out the

side of his mouth. "What's the matter, the adorable little zombie isn't hungry? Poor baby. Maybe you want to gnaw on my arm for an appetizer?"

Bill's eyes flashed as he stared at his son. "That's enough, Lester. You know that's nonsense, made up by silly Hollywood movies."

"How would I know that?" protested Lester. "It's not like I've met a bunch of zombies before. I mean, are you serious? I didn't even know they actually existed!"

"They exist," said Jenny, quietly but firmly.

Everyone ate in silence for a few moments.

"I would have a terribly adverse reaction if I ate anything other than jelly beans," I told Lester.

"That's random," Lester mumbled, picking at his food. "So how long is this . . . *thing* going to be staying with us, anyway?"

Jenny looked at her husband, then took a deep breath. "All we know for sure is that he'll be staying with us for the time being."

"I don't *get it*," moaned Lester. "Where did he come from? Why is he here? What are you trying to prove?"

"All good questions, son," Bill said. "The only one I can address right now is why. And the answer is, because it's the right thing to do."

Lester thumped his glass down with an angry clatter. "You gotta be KIDDING me!"

"Would you prefer we send him away?" said Bill. "Do you know how hard it would be for him to survive on his own?"

I could answer that one. Very hard. As in, *impossibly* hard.

Lester threw up his hands. "Why not just turn him in?"

Bill looked at his son with a gentle but stern expression. "Because he's done nothing wrong."

"Your father and I have discussed it," said Jenny. "Norbus needs our help. We're going to make sure he feels at home here."

"ZOMBIES DON'T EVEN *LIVE* IN HOMES!" bellowed Lester.

Bill placed his fork down on his plate and looked across the table at his son. Everything suddenly got very quiet. I think even the crickets stopped chirping.

"They do now," Bill said.

"Don't be shy," Jenny said to me. "Eat your supper."

I looked at this woman and this man. Why was a voice inside my head telling me that humans were the enemy? These humans did not seem like the enemy.

I picked up a fire-engine-red jelly bean and popped it in my mouth.

It tasted good.

WHO I AM IS NOT WHO I NEED TO BE

The next morning I was sitting at the kitchen table, eating green jelly beans, when Bill came in. "Good morning, Norbus," he said. "Did you sleep well?"

"No," I said.

Bill shook his head. "Oh right," he said, laughing softly.

After breakfast, Jenny led me to a couch in the living room. "Now, Norbus, we have some work to do."

"What kind of work?"

"Well, Bill and I are trying to figure out exactly where to go from here, with this whole situation. But that's going to take some time, and in the meantime, powerful people are looking for you. We don't want to arouse suspicion, but we also don't want to hide you away like a prisoner in our own home." She looked right at me with her kind eyes. "So, we're going to treat you as a member of our family. Which means you need to learn how to do things that any kid would do in any family." She saw my clueless expression and smiled gently. "Nothing scary or weird, I promise. Just normal, everyday activities, like staying clean, getting dressed, and going to school."

When she said *school*, I stopped breathing for a second.

Or, I would have, if I actually breathed.

"You want me to attend school?"

"That's right." Jenny put her hand on my shoulder. It was warm. Humans are so warm, in general. "You didn't ask to be put on this earth, but now that you're here, you have every right to live a normal life, and we want to help you do that."

"GROSS!" Lester came barging into the room, pointing at me and sneering. "He's wearing the same clothes he wore yesterday!"

"Well, of course he is," said Jenny. "They're the only clothes he has."

She looked at me, and I shrugged apologetically. Jenny had tried to get me to change into pajamas the night before, but I'd refused. I'd never worn anything but the yellow shirt, blue pants, and orange ID tag I was (re)born with.

But now, Jenny was saying I would have to start not just

Protective goggles

Sharp teeth for non-jellybean food

Cool kid camouflage

wearing typical human clothes but acting like a typical human.

Is there such a thing as a typical human?

"Are you ready to get started, Norbus?" asked Jenny. "You'll do great."

I stood up. "I'm ready."

Lester glared at me. "You might learn how to *act* like a

human," he sneered, "but you will never *be* a human." Then he walked out of the room and slammed the door.

I decided right then and there that I would be a Bill and Jenny kind of person and not a Lester kind of person.

"Before we get started, there's one thing we need to do," Jenny said. Then she placed a small box on the table.

"What's that?" I asked her.

"Contact lenses." She opened the box and took out a tiny blue lens, which she held up for me to see. "You're going to need to put these in your eyes," she said. "They will turn your eyes blue."

I was confused. "Why do I need to turn my eyes blue?" Jenny looked at me, and I immediately understood. "Oh right."

Jenny sighed. "I know this isn't who you are," she said. "But unfortunately, it's who you need to be."

THE REAL WORLd

"We're going to *what*?!?" Lester howled.

It was two days later, in the middle of my human training. (So far I'd gotten pretty good at brushing my teeth but was having a little trouble tying my shoes.) Lester was sitting at the kitchen table, moaning to his mom. I was on the porch, pretending not to listen to the whole thing.

"We're going to take Norbus on a few errands," Jenny said, answering her son. "He needs to get some clothes at the mall. Besides, it's time for him to experience what it's like out there in the real world. And I'd like you to come with us."

Lester looked like his eyes were going to pop out of his head. "As *IF*! What if my friends see me?"

"The world won't end," said Jenny. "You'll just have to trust me on that one."

"Fine," muttered Lester. "But I want to get the new DangerRanger X-3000 or I'm not going."

Jenny sighed. "We'll talk about it in the car."

"What's DangerRanger X-3000?" I asked, wondering what kind of item could possibly hold such power over Lester.

"The greatest game ever," Lester said.

"The end of civilization as we know it," Jenny said.

I wasn't sure how they could both be right, but I decided not to ask.

Our first stop was the grocery store, which was an enormous building that seemed to go on forever.

"This is where we buy our food for the week," Jenny explained.

There were a ton of people walking around, and they all had big metal baskets on wheels, filled to the brim with lots of things that I guess they were going to eat, although I wasn't sure how people could consume all that food in a whole lifetime, much less in seven days.

"Why are there fifteen different kinds of peanut butter?" I asked Jenny.

"I have no idea," she answered.

😖 😎 😃

As we walked up and down the aisles, I could tell that people were looking at me. I was wearing some of Lester's old clothes that Bill had found in the attic—a pair of jeans that were way too big, and a yellow T-shirt with a picture of a monkey surfing on the front. The shirt said LIFE'S A BEACH, whatever that meant.

Lester pointed at a box that said SWEET-A-RAMAS. "That's the ticket!" he announced, picking up the box and throwing it into our cart.

"What is that?" I asked.

"Only the best cereal in the entire world, that's what," Lester said.

But Jenny shook her head and put the box back on the shelf. "Absolutely not. That stuff is pure sugar."

"MOM!" Lester peered at his mother. "Do you want me to stand up on top of this cart and yell 'zombie'?"

She glared at him, then threw the box back in the cart.

Lester looked at me and almost smiled.

When our cart was full, we headed to the front of the store to pay. Ahead of us in line was a small boy who was standing there with his father.

The boy looked up at me. "What's wrong with you?" he asked.

I glanced at Jenny, then back at the boy. "Nothing is wrong with me, I am perfectly well."

"Oh," said the boy. "You look like you're sick or something."

The boy's father bent down. "Now, Sammy, let's not be rude," he whispered. "Leave the boy alone." But then the father looked at me, and I could tell he thought the same thing. "Let's go to another register," he said. "I'm sure these nice people don't want to be bothered."

I didn't know what to say, so I didn't say anything. But Jenny sure did. "You don't have to go to another register," she said to them. "And he is not sick. He is just fine. Good day to you both." She looked at Lester and me. "Let's go, boys. We'll shop later."

"But the Sweet-A-Ramas!" whined Lester.

Jenny shook her head. "Not today," she said. "We'll come back some other time."

Lester shot a look my way.

No almost-smile this time.

☹ 😎 😄

Once we were back in the car, Jenny turned to me. "We're going to the mall to get you some clothes," she said, "and that's all there is to it." I waited for Lester to moan and groan, but there must have been something in her tone that made him keep his complaints to himself.

The mall was even bigger than the grocery store. The inside was like a giant body with arms everywhere, and every arm was a brightly lit, really loud room that had clothing, or toys, or electronic gadgets, or shoes, or—for some reason—people painting other people's nails.

"I'm heading over to GameTown," Lester announced.

Jenny shook her head. "Not yet you're not," she said. "I'm going to run and get a quick cup of coffee. Just help Norbus in the store for a minute; I'll be right there."

"Ugh!" Lester started walking way ahead of me, and I hurried to catch up. "This way," he said, and headed toward a store called Kidz Cloze. When we walked inside, I had to squint because the lights were so bright. The shelves were filled with shirts, pants, sweaters, sweatshirts, and jackets, of all shapes, sizes, and colors.

"Why are there fifteen different kinds of jeans?" I asked Lester.

"The same reason there are fifteen different kinds of peanut butter," he answered.

We wandered around for a minute or so, until a girl who looked about the same age as Lester walked up to us. She had blue hair and was wearing jeans with about a million rips in them.

"Why doesn't she get all those holes in her pants fixed?" I asked Lester.

"That's the style, dummy."

"Why is there a pin through her nose?"

"Stop asking questions."

The girl gave us a bored smile. "Can I help you guys?" Then she noticed Lester and her smile became slightly less bored. "Oh, hey, Lester."

Lester's cheeks turned bright red.

I had no idea human faces could change colors like that.

"Oh, hey, Darlene, what's going on?" Lester said, in a super friendly tone of voice. "I didn't know you worked here."

Blue-haired Darlene's face didn't turn red at all. "Yup, for the last two months," she said. "Trying to make some extra cash, you know how it is."

"Oh, absolutely, I sure do," said Lester. Then he laughed awkwardly.

This was a new side of Lester.

Darlene looked down at me. "Who's this guy?" she asked Lester. "Is he, like, related to you or something?"

Lester looked panicked at the prospect of trying to explain who I was. "He . . . uh . . ."

But before he could finish, Darlene bent down to take a closer look at me. "You are one cool-looking little dude," she said. "I would *kill* for silky skin like that. It would take a serious amount of pricey makeup that I totally can't afford."

"Okay," I said. Then, remembering the manners Jenny had been teaching me, I added, "Oh, and thank you very much for your gracious words."

She examined my face. "So you must, like, never go out in the sun, right?"

"It would be neither wise nor prudent," I answered, which made Lester roll his eyes.

Darlene pulled her phone out of a ripped jean pocket. "And those cheekbones! Seriously, you could, like, model if you wanted. Mind if I grab a quick selfie?" She stuck her face next to mine and took a picture. "Totally posting this."

It was at that point that Lester decided he wanted to

rejoin the conversation. "So, yeah, he's my cousin from, uh, out of town. Great kid," he said.

I looked at him, confused.

He looked back at me and whispered, "Mind your own business, and no one gets hurt."

Darlene stared at her phone and typed something at lightning speed. "That's awesome!" she said. "This pic is going to blow up. I'm going to get, like, a thousand likes."

I had absolutely no idea what she was talking about. It barely sounded like English, to be honest.

"Anyway, Darlene," Lester said, "my cousin is going to be staying with us for a while, in case you ever want to come over and hang out."

"That could be cool, maybe next week," Darlene said. She looked at me. "What's your name, anyway?"

Now it was my turn to stand there awkwardly, but luckily Jenny walked up right at that moment.

"Oh, hi, Darlene. We're just looking for some new school clothes. Can you point us in the right direction?"

"Hey, Mrs. Kinder. Yeah, right this way." She put her arm around my shoulder. "By the time I'm done with him, he'll be the flashiest-looking kid in town."

As Darlene led me away, I glanced back at Lester.

"Are you coming?" I asked. "Your help would be extremely beneficial."

He caught up to us and gave me a light smack on the back.

It was the first non-mean thing he'd ever done to me.

I ended up getting three shirts, a jacket, a sweatshirt, and two different kinds of jeans. They were all too big, but I was the only one who seemed to care.

"The pants are falling down," I said to Lester. "And the belt barely helps."

"Exactly," he said.

gIRLS

That night, as I was going to bed (but not to sleep), Lester came into my room. "So at the mall, today . . . uh, yeah," he said. "That was, you know."

I looked at him. "I'm sorry, I'm unable to comprehend what you're saying."

"Dude, listen." Lester let out a big sigh. "You did me a solid at the mall today, with Darlene. I've been trying to land some eye-time with her for a dog's age, if you know what I mean."

Again, I shook my head. "Again I apologize, but in fact, I don't know what you mean. Is there any way you could express yourself in a somewhat more coherent fashion?"

"I like her, okay?!" Lester fell back on my bed. "I've always liked Darlene, but she never gave me the time of day, until today. And that's thanks to you. For some reason, she thinks you're, like, completely awesome."

"Ah, I see." I watched him as he lay there. "Will you be sleeping in my bed tonight?" I asked. "If so, I can find an alternate place to lie down."

"Of course not." He yawned loudly, then stretched his arms up practically to the ceiling. "I just figured, since you did me that solid today, I'd do you one back."

"What's a solid?"

"Like, a favor. I'm going to do you a favor."

"That's sounds very nice, thank you," I told Lester. "What is this favor?"

Lester pulled himself up to a sitting position. "I'm going to give you two very important pieces of advice. One, loosen up. You're so serious you give me the creeps. And two, you need to stop talking like Albert Freakin' Einstein."

"Who Freakin' Who?"

"Don't worry about it." Lester got up. "So what's the deal with the fancy vocabulary, anyway? Why do you use big words all the time?"

"I don't know," I told him. "Ever since I can remember, I've spoken like this. I guess I was born that way."

"I thought you weren't born at all," Lester said.

"Oh, yes, good point. Thank you for the advice; I will be sure to be more careful with my vernacular."

Lester pointed his finger right at me. "See, there! That word, *vernacular*. There is absolutely no need to use that word." He paused. "What does it mean, anyway?"

"Well, it means the way people speak."

"Then fine, say that," Lester said. "Say 'I need to be more careful with the way I speak.'"

"Okay."

"I know my parents have been trying to help you, but take it from me: If you're going to go to school, you need to act like everyone else and talk like everyone else."

"Okay."

Lester took out the same phone that everyone seemed to have, stared at it for no apparent reason, and then put it back in his pocket. (He did this approximately 8,483 times a day.) "No more words over three syllables," he said.

"I'll try, but that seems both unrealistic and inflexible, to be honest."

"What did I just say?"

"Oh right. My apologies."

"You mean you're sorry."

"Right, I'm sorry."

"Yeesh, you've got a lot to learn," Lester said. "Or unlearn, I guess." His phone buzzed, and he yanked it out again to read it. "Yo, it's Darlene! She says it was fun running into me at the mall!"

"What a felicitous text indeed," I said before I could stop myself.

He glared at me.

"That was a joke," I claimed. "I'm loosening up."

"You've got a ways to go, pal," Lester said, and he had a very good point.

mEETiN9 ARNOLd

Finally it was the day before my first day of school. I'd gotten semi-used to the new clothes and the contact lenses, and I'd even taken two showers, which were not enjoyable at all.

I was outside on the front porch, watching the clouds go by, when I felt a hand on my shoulder. "Come with me, Norbus," Bill said. "We need to have a talk."

I followed him into the room they called the TV room, probably because it had a giant TV in it. I'd watched a show with Bill and Jenny the night before. First, all these people sang really loudly, and then other people decided if the singers were good at singing or not, and then the singers would either jump up and down happily or cry like it was the worst day of their lives.

It was very strange.

But what's even stranger is that I'd enjoyed the show very much.

"Are we watching more TV?" I asked Bill.

"Absolutely not," he answered, with a laugh. "There's only so much of that silliness I can take."

We sat down on the couch. "What did you want to talk about?" I asked, even though a part of me knew the answer.

"I wanted to tell you a little bit about where you came from," Bill said. Then he sat there, as if waiting for me to say something, but I didn't have anything to say.

Bill took a deep breath. "The human regeneration program has been in development for about three years. Anyone who knows about it will go to jail if they reveal its existence to the outside world."

"How do *you* know about it?"

"I wish I could tell you that," he said, "but I can't. But I can say that you and the other zombies escaped through a breach of security on the southern border of the Territory."

I stared at him without blinking. "What's the Territory?"

A look of surprise came over Bill's face. "That's where you're from, Norbus," he said. "Where you were developed, and studied, and kept." He let that sink in for a second. "From what we understand," he continued, "all the other escapees were rounded up and subjected to something called the Salt Melt, which causes paralysis in regenerated humans. They were then returned to the Territory."

That explained the man chasing me with the bag of salt in his hands.

"Luckily, we found you before they did," he added, softly.

"I see." I could feel a pounding in my chest, almost as if my heart were actually beating. "Thank you for telling me."

Bill put his hand on my shoulder. I could feel the warmth through my shirt. "I wish I could say that this project was for a good reason, and if we returned you, you would be protected," he said. "But as of right now, we don't believe that to be the case. And until I find out for sure, you're going to stay right here where we can look after you."

There was a buzzing in my ears, like the sound of the microwave that Jenny uses to heat up her coffee. "Can I . . . uh . . . why is it so hard for me to remember anything before the escape?"

Bill shrugged gently. "Well, I don't believe you were designed to have much of a memory. And when you fell into that ditch, you avoided being captured, but you also got a good knock on the head. Might have knocked the few memories you did have clear out of you."

"Oh," I said.

"I'm very sorry, Norbus."

I didn't have much to say after that. I didn't feel sad, or nervous, or scared.

I just felt alone.

Bill stood up. "Now, as I've said, no one knows you're here with us, and I'd like to keep it that way. Which is where the next part of our conversation comes in." He walked over to a large bookshelf that was above the TV and pulled down a book. "This is a little awkward, but I have to ask you something. Can you read?"

I blinked. "Can I read?"

"That's right." Bill opened up the book. "Now, I know you have a strong vocabulary, so you're obviously very bright, but I have no idea if you're a reader." He looked down, a little embarrassed by the conversation. "Are you, son?"

"I don't know," I told him. "I can't remember."

"Well, let's find out, shall we? Why don't you go on over and pick out a book."

I picked up a book called *War and Peace*. It was so heavy it practically fell out of my hands.

"Seriously?" said Bill. "Why that one?"

"I don't know," I said again.

"You might want to—" began Bill, but he didn't finish his sentence, because by then I was already flipping the pages as fast as I could.

Sixty seconds later, I looked up. "This isn't really my kind of book, to tell you the truth."

Bill glanced down at the page I was on and his eyes went wide. "Are you trying to tell me you just read forty-seven pages?"

I nodded. "It's clear that the author is a great writer, but all those Russian names are very confusing."

As I struggled to put the heavy book back on the shelf, Bill laughed. "Well! I knew you all were smart, but I guess I didn't realize quite *how* smart."

I suddenly felt shy and stared down at my hands. They looked incredibly white, and you could practically see right through to the bones. Now that I was seeing humans up close all the time, with their deep, rich coloring, I realized how completely different we were.

"Anyway, Norbus, there's a reason why I asked you about reading." Bill held up the book he'd been holding in his hand. "This is a book of names. I'd like to find you a new name, one that won't draw any unwanted attention. A more normal name."

"I think my name *is* normal."

"I think you know what I mean."

After a few seconds, I shrugged. "Any name is fine."

"I'd like you to pick it out." Bill brought the book over to me. "Now remember, this is the name you're going to live with, possibly even for the rest of your days. You need to find something that makes you comfortable."

"Okay." I wanted to get this over with as quickly as possible, so I turned to the first page of the book and pointed without even looking. "That one."

He peered down. "Arnold? You want your first name to be Arnold?"

"Yes."

"Fine. Arnold Kinder it is."

I was confused. "Kinder? What's wrong with Clacknozzle?"

He sighed. "Again, it will just make you stick out like a sore thumb. We don't want that."

"But I *am* a sore thumb," I said. "I won't fit in, no matter how hard I try. I don't look like you, and I never will. I look like me."

"Norbus," said Bill in a gentle voice, "I realize how difficult this must be for you. But I want to assure you of one thing. This is all just to make life easier for you. Yes, you have to fit in to our society, but that doesn't mean you're giving up your true identity. And it doesn't mean you have to stop being who you really are."

I looked at him, feeling the heat of my red eyes burning through my cold white skin. "I don't have to give up my true identity?"

"Absolutely not."

"Fine." I handed the book back to Bill. "Then I would like my last name to be Zombie."

Bill laughed, in a short, loud burst. "HA!" But then he looked at me, and he realized I was serious. "Norbus, you can read a thousand-page novel without breaking a sweat. I would think someone with your level of intelligence knows why that can't happen. And besides, we are going to tell people you're related to us; so obviously, your last name should be Kinder. Surely you understand."

I did understand, of course. But I didn't care. After a while, you realize which are the things that matter. The things that are important enough to make you say to yourself, *Without this, nothing is worth fighting for.*

"You said I don't have to stop being who I really am."

"That is true," Bill admitted.

"Well, this is who I am."

Neither of us said anything for a few seconds, then I had an idea. "How about if we spell it differently? Z-O-M-B-E-E. That way, no one will suspect anything."

"You can't really believe that."

"It's what I want."

"You are one stubborn young man."

We both stared at each other for a few seconds. Then I said, "Okay then, how about this: We'll make my middle initial Z, and my last name O-M-B-E-E?"

Bill threw up his hands. "For gosh sakes, we may as well keep Clacknozzle!"

"Somebody else named me Clacknozzle," I told him, "so now that I think about it, that's not who I really am either.

You said I get to name myself this time. Well, I would like my last name to be Ombee." I paused for a second, then added, "That's my final offer."

Bill looked at me like he was both annoyed and impressed. We both knew how silly it sounded. We both knew how crazy it was. And we both knew that there was no way I was going to change my mind.

Bill stuck out his hand, and I shook it. Then he patted me on the back.

"Nice to meet you, Arnold Z. Ombee."

March 3, 2027
GT 278
PROJECT Z
THE OUTER BRANCH
ARIZONA

ATTENTION ALL UNITS: The search continues for the last remaining escapee of the breach that occurred on February 25, 2027.

The subject, Z-designated Norbus Clacknozzle, is a juvenile male. While there have been some clues to his whereabouts, such as footsteps and traces of *sudoris zombutam* along a dirt road west of the freeway near the mall, there have been no confirmed sightings.

As it is urgent and mandatory that the general population remains unaware of PROJECT Z, there have been no public announcements of any kind that allude to the breach or the escaped subject.

All units will continue to search and patrol the area until further notice.

Horace Brantley
Regional Commander, National Martial Services

THE FIRST DAY

"Are you ready?" asked Bill.

I wasn't sure how to answer that.

Is a zombie ever really ready for fifth grade?

When I went downstairs that morning, after spending the night in my room thinking and reading, the first thing I saw was a note from Jenny.

> Had to go to work. Look forward to a full report tonight. Aunt Jenny.

I stuck the note in the pocket of my brand-new, incredibly uncomfortable shirt.

Bill was in the kitchen, making breakfast for Lester. When he saw me, he clapped his hands together. "Holy smokes,

Norbus—I mean, Arnold—you look great!" He walked over and handed me my notebook. "Are you ready? Are you feeling okay? Did you get some rest? Do you need anything? Are all your supplies in your backpack? Did you remember your pencils? Do you want to go over everything again?"

I took a deep breath. "Maybe one more time."

Bill sat down in front of me.

"Who are you?"

"I'm Arnold Z. Ombee, your nephew, and I'm here because my parents had to move overseas for six months."

"Why are you so pale?"

"I have a skin condition and can't go in the sun."

"Why can't you play sports?"

"I have a muscle mass deficiency."

"Why can't you eat most foods?"

"Allergies."

"Do you have your doctor's note?"

I got the note out of my pocket and unfolded it.

I looked up at Bill. "Who's Doctor Jonas again?"

Please excuse Arnold Ombee from strenuous gym activity. He can't run because one of his heart valves is leaking. Sincerely, Doctor Irving Jonas

"A family friend."

"Oh."

He smiled. "All righty, then. People are going to think you should be in a plastic bubble, but that's okay." He was trying to make a joke, but I could tell how worried he was.

"I'll be fine," I told him. "I will."

The truth was, I was scared.

"You'll be great, I know it," Bill said. "And if you get nervous, just take a few deep breaths, it will calm you right down."

"Uh, okay." I didn't have the heart to remind him that I don't breathe. At all. Ever.

Lester started drumming his hands impatiently on the table. "Let's GO! We're gonna miss the BUS! Come on, *Arnold Z. Ombee*." He said it like it was the dumbest name ever.

He may have had a point.

Bill gave me a big hug. I felt my cold bones melt a little in his arms.

"Go get 'em," he said.

Lester held the door open as we walked outside. He quickly caught up to me and smacked the notebook out of my hands. As I bent down to pick it up, he leaned over me. I could smell the Sweet-A-Ramas on his breath. "Get used to people doing stuff like that to you," he said. "You're the new kid, and you've got a target on your back."

"Okay."

"And remember, I'm in ninth grade and you're in fifth," he said. "So as soon as we get off the bus, you're on your own. Here's my advice: Keep your head down and don't make anyone mad. And remember, no fancy words! Got it? If someone figures out who you are, you're as good as dead."

"Don't you mean undead?" I asked him, trying to impress him with another joke—but he was already running, far ahead of me, and he didn't look back.

KiKi, GHOSTiE, ANd THE FLiCKER

The school bus was the scariest place I have ever been in my kind-of life. And I'm a zombie. I'm supposed to specialize in scary.

Lester ran straight to the back of the bus, where the older kids were. When I got on, the first person I saw was the driver. He didn't look at me so that was okay. But then I turned and started walking down the aisle, and I suddenly felt like I was under a very unfriendly microscope. Kids stared at me with challenging eyes, as if they were daring me to try and sit next to them, just so they could tell me to get lost. Boys were elbowing one another, snickering and whispering stuff like "Get a load of the new kid" and "Looks like he moved here from Losertown."

And the girls? Believe it or not, they were even worse.

They refused to look at me at all.

I felt sweat start to ooze out of my shoes as I walked up

and down the aisle. Then for a few seconds I just stood there, trying to figure out what to do.

"Take a seat, dork," I heard a voice say. "We can't go until you sit down." I realized the voice was right: The bus wasn't moving, and all the heads had swiveled toward me, waiting.

Suddenly out of nowhere, I saw a girl move a few inches to her left. *Was that an invitation?*

I decided it was.

I dashed forward and plopped down next to the girl, who didn't even glance at me. I leaned back, but it wasn't very comfortable. Something was in the way.

"Your backpack," said the girl, still staring straight ahead. "Take it off and put it under your seat."

I did what I was told.

"Thanks," I said. "This is my first day."

"Duh," said the girl.

I snuck a quick peek in her direction. Her skin was as dark as mine was light. She was wearing a blue dress and blue shoes. She also had a blue barrette in her hair.

"Do you like blue?" I asked her, like an idiot.

She covered her mouth and let out a short giggle. "Duh again."

"My name is Arnold Z. Ombee," I said, just to see how it sounded.

It sounded not so good.

The girl twirled her hair and let out a short, loud laugh. "That's your name, seriously?"

"You can just call me Arnold," I said, deciding then and there to only use my first name from that point on. "Thank you for making room for me so I could sit here. That was very magnanimous of you."

"Very what?"

I silently yelled at myself for using a four-syllable word. "It was nice of you. Very nice."

"Oh. Yeah, it *was* nice, you're right." She turned her head and looked at me for the first time. "Why are you so pale?"

That's when a normal human boy would blush. But not me.

"I— I have this skin condition where if I'm in the sun too long, I break out in terrible rashes and hives. It's like an allergy. So I stay indoors most of the time." Like my name, the explanation had sounded a lot better at home; now that I was saying it out loud to a real live actual human girl, it felt extremely—what's the word Lester would use?—oh, yes. Uncool.

I waited for the girl to laugh in my face, but instead she just shrugged. "Oh, I'm sorry. That's too bad. I love being outside. My name's Kiki." She looked out the window and started singing to herself.

"What song is that?" I asked, but she just smiled.

I took that as a sign that the conversation was over.

The girl named Kiki kept singing, and I was minding my own business, waiting for the bus ride to end, when I felt a flick on the back of my neck. I ignored it, thinking I must have imagined it, until I felt it again, a little harder this time. It was definitely a flick all right, caused by a human finger.

I turned around.

A boy was sitting there by himself. His face was red, his eyes were little slits of blue, and his black hair stood up in short, angry spikes.

"Yo," said the boy. "What are you looking at?"

"Well, you're flicking my neck with your finger, and I'd like you to stop it, please."

"You'd like me to stop it??" He stood up. "Did you hear that, everybody? Ghostie here would like me to stop it!"

"My name is Arnold," I said, trying to sound convincing.

The red-faced boy snickered. "Yeah, but you're white as a ghost, so Ghostie it is."

"Hey!" rumbled the bus driver. "Knock it off back there."

The boy sat back down, and I turned back around to face the front. I glanced over at Kiki, hoping for a little smile that might make me feel better, but she was still looking out the window and humming.

FLICK!

It was the hardest one of all.

"Ghostie!" the Flicker said. "Why is your skin so cold?"

But before I could give him another rehearsed answer—*I have a circulatory issue, my blood pumps more slowly than normal people*—Kiki turned around and flashed her brown eyes at the Flicker.

"What?" he moaned, suddenly looking guilty.

"Stop calling him Ghostie," she said. "He said his name is Arnold." Then she looked at me and winked. "Right, Ghostie?"

The good news was, everyone laughed, including the Flicker, and I didn't have to worry anymore that I was going to get beat up before the first day of school even started.

The bad news was, I had a new nickname.

WELCOME TO THE NEIGHBORHOOD

"Can I have everyone's attention?" the teacher said. "We have a new young man in school today. Let's make him feel welcome."

Well, if *that* isn't an invitation to make fun of someone, I don't know what is.

I was standing in the front of the classroom, having just handed my principal's note to the teacher. The teacher's name was Irma Huggle, which made me wonder why I had to change my name from Norbus Clacknozzle.

"Please give a warm Bernard J. Frumpstein Elementary School hello to"—Mrs. Huggle glanced down at the note— "Arnold Z. Ombee. Spelled O-M-B-E-E."

At the announcement of my "name," the other kids—who had been slouched over, barely looking at me—suddenly sat up straight as arrows and started murmuring a mile a minute.

"Ombee?"

"Is he serious?"

"What kind of name is that?"

"Shush!" commanded Mrs. Huggle. She gave me a friendly smile, which made me feel better. "Please take the open seat next to Mr. Brantley."

I glanced over to where she was pointing. Care to guess who Mr. Brantley was?

You got it. The Flicker.

I walked slowly to my seat. The Flicker was grinning like he'd just won the lottery, which, according to the commercials I'd seen on television, was a very good thing. Everyone else was staring at me with their mouths open, as if the combination of a new kid, a weird name, and see-through skin was too much to take. I couldn't blame them. I would have been fascinated and a little creeped out by me, too.

"Hey, Ghostie," said a girl's voice, and I glanced over. Kiki, my seatmate on the bus, was in the row in front of me, smiling.

"Hi, Kiki," I said. I pointed at the Flicker. "Should I ask the teacher if I can move?"

"Only if you want to immediately become known as the wimpiest wimp in the class." She giggled. "Anyway, Evan's harmless. We've been friends since, like, forever."

"You have?" I glanced over at the Flicker—whose name was apparently Evan—and suddenly he didn't seem so bad.

"Yup," she said. "Anyway, find me at lunch."

A weird feeling filled my body—but not a bad weird feeling, a good weird feeling. "Okay, I will." I noticed Kiki was humming to herself again. "Why are you always singing?"

She shrugged. "I'm not sure. Maybe because it makes me happy, or maybe because I'm always happy. One or the other."

I thought about that for a second. I wasn't sure what being happy felt like. Maybe someday I could be happy, too.

Then I sat down, just in time for Evan to flick me in the neck one last time.

"Looks like we're neighbors!" he exclaimed, still grinning that grin.

That did not make me happy.

CRUTCH

As soon as I realized that you were supposed to raise your hand if you knew the answer to a question, I raised my hand whenever Mrs. Huggle asked one.

"Yes, Arnold?" Mrs. Huggle would say.

"The capital of North Dakota is Bismarck."

"Very good."

A few minutes later, I realized that if you raise your hand every time the teacher asks a question, and you actually know the right answer, the other kids will find you irritating and obnoxious.

That was the end of me raising my hand.

"Hey, Ghostie," Evan whispered. "How did you get to be such a genius?"

I couldn't tell him the answer—because I didn't know the answer—so instead I just said, "I read a lot."

"That's gross," Evan said, and it took me a minute to realize he was talking about reading.

I decided to change the subject. "Why do you all call me Ghostie?"

Evan snorted. "Are you serious?"

"Yes, I am."

"I mean, look at you. You're so pale you're practically invisible. You look like you could walk through walls. Not to mention you're a pretty scary-looking dude."

I looked down at myself. He wasn't wrong.

The next thing I knew, there was a sudden commotion on the other side of the classroom. A small girl wearing a shirt with a horse on it and pink ribbons in her hair suddenly let out a scream and threw a book on the ground. A tall adult woman who wore thick red glasses was sitting next to the girl, and she quickly bent over and picked up the book. When the girl cried out again, the adult woman took her out of the room.

"Who's that?" I asked Evan.

"That's Sarah Anne," he said. "She used to be in Special Ed. She never talks, either because she can't or she doesn't want to, I'm not really sure. But I heard she's really smart."

"Wow, that must be hard."

"Yeah. And sometimes Sarah Anne gets really upset for no reason, or no reason anyone can figure out, anyways. Which is why Ms. Frawley is always with her."

A boy, who wore his hat backward for some reason, suddenly leaned over. "Yo, Crutch, you finally found a friend? Keep it down, I'm trying to learn stuff."

People snickered, and Evan sunk down in his seat.

"Why did that kid call you Crutch?"

Evan glared at me. "The same reason I call you Ghostie, dummy." He pointed underneath his desk. He was wearing shorts, and I noticed his right leg was a slightly darker color than his left leg. Then I realized why. Evan had an artificial leg.

"Because we're different from everyone else," Evan said.

LUNCH

On my way to lunch, two boys cornered me in the hallway near the gym. One boy was the backward hat kid who had called Evan "Crutch." The other boy was really tall and had long hair and freckles.

"Hey, Arnold," said the backward hat one. "Is your middle initial really Z and your last name really Ombee? Like, zombie?"

I hesitated. I know humans are good at lying, but zombies are not. We're extremely honest.

It's an underappreciated trait.

"What kind of a question is that?" I asked the kid with the backward hat. He looked confused by my answer— which was the opposite of an answer, actually—and I don't blame him.

He poked me in the chest. "Whaddya mean, what kind of question is that? It's the kind that wants an answer!" The

two boys leaned forward, and I found myself backed up against a metal locker.

"Yes, I'm an Ombee!" I blurted out. "I don't care if you make fun of my name because of what it sounds like! I'm proud to be an Ombee, and I don't care who knows it!"

They stared at me in shock.

"Now please let me through. Kiki is waiting for me at lunch."

"Ha!" said Backward Hat. "No one is waiting for you!" But they slowly backed up. As I started walking away, Backward

Hat reached out and grabbed my arm. I could feel the heat of his hand through my shirt. I wondered if he could feel the chill of my skin.

"I'm proud to be a Klepsaw," he said, his voice barely above a whisper. "And don't you ever forget it."

"Ghostie! Come sit with us!"

I was on one side of the cafeteria, standing with a tray full of food I wasn't going to eat, and not sure where to sit. Kiki was sitting at a table right in the middle, with a bunch of other girls and boys.

"Ghostie! What are you, a statue?"

"There's no room," I told her.

Kiki smacked the shoulder of the boy sitting next to her. "Simon, slide over! Arnold needs a place to sit!"

The boy named Simon didn't say anything, he just moved down. Kiki smiled brightly at me and patted the seat. "All yours!"

It occurred to me right then and there that Kiki was a good person to be friends with.

"Thanks for letting me sit here," I said to Kiki.

"Do you hate it when I call you Ghostie?" she asked. "I won't do it anymore if you don't want me to."

"I don't mind," I said. Ghostie was no different from Arnold, really. Neither one was my name.

"So what's your story, Arnold Z. Ombee?" Kiki asked. "What does the Z stand for? Where did you move from? Do you like music? Do you play sports? Do you have any brothers and sisters? What's your favorite color? Why are you so skinny? What's the deal with your last name?"

All the other kids at the table had stopped talking. In fact, I think all the other kids in the whole cafeteria had stopped talking. They were waiting for my answers.

"I . . . uh . . . my parents had to go away for a while because of their jobs, so I moved in with my aunt and uncle. I don't know where the name comes from."

The backward hat kid, who was sitting at the end of the table, leaned in. "Are they spies?" he asked. "You're probably going to tell us that they're, like, secret agents or something."

"Who?"

"Your parents."

Uh-oh. I hadn't rehearsed that question with Bill and Jenny. I froze.

"Yeah, are they?" asked a girl who had painted her fingernails blue for some reason. "Are they, like, on some special assignment that no one can know about?"

Remember I said that thing about how honest zombies are?

Well, that doesn't mean we can't be a little misleading when necessary.

"I can't talk about my family," I explained to everyone at the table. "It's too risky."

"Wait a sec, they're really spies?" Kiki exclaimed. "That is so cool! So, is, like, Ombee a fake name, to throw people off?"

"Something like that," I said.

"Holy smokes," said the kid with the backward hat. "Tell us everything."

I smiled but shook my head. "I really can't talk about it."

Which, of course, made all the kids desperate to talk about it.

They started asking me all sorts of questions, and even though I only responded with grunts and half-answers, all of a sudden I was Arnold Z. Ombee, the mysterious new kid, son of the shadowy Ombee spy family.

It was pretty awesome there for a second.

And then it wasn't.

"I don't believe you," said a voice sitting two tables away.

Everyone stopped chattering and looked over. Evan Brantley was eating lunch by himself.

"Evan!" Kiki exclaimed. "How many times do I have to tell you to stop sitting over there! Come over here with us!"

"I'd rather not," Evan said.

"Please?" begged Kiki.

"He said he didn't want to," said Backward Hat.

Kiki gave the kid a dirty look. "Stop being a jerk."

Backward Hat looked wounded and decided to take it out on Evan. "Go back to eating your grody lunch," he sneered.

I noticed that Evan was eating something green and gloopy. It did look pretty disgusting, I had to admit.

"It just so happens I have a lot of allergies," Evan said. "And I have a sensitive stomach."

He sounds like me, I thought to myself, *except for real*.

"At least you HAVE a stomach, Crutch," said the tall, long-haired boy. "More than I can say for some of your other body parts."

"That's not funny!" barked Kiki, but everyone laughed. Evan stared down at his gloopy green food. Then he looked back up, but instead of glaring at the kid with the long hair, he glared at me.

"I don't believe your story, Ghostie," Evan said. "Or Arnold, or whatever your actual name is."

I looked at Evan, sitting alone, and suddenly realized why he kept flicking me on the back of the neck during the bus ride to school. He was looking for attention. He was looking for a friend.

Because except for Kiki, he didn't have any.

As for me, I was surrounded by kids who wanted to know more about me, and it seemed like I could have a bunch of new friends right then and there, if I wanted to. On the very first day of school! It would have been such a relief. And the Kinders would have been so happy for me.

But for some reason, none of that mattered.

I got up and walked over to Evan's table. "Do you mind if I sit here? Then you can ask me more questions I'm not allowed to answer."

Evan blinked up at me. "Really? Uh . . . sure."

Backward Hat snorted. "You know what? He's probably

not a spy at all. He's just a pasty little know-it-all with a stupid name!"

Other kids started jabbering in agreement, and it seemed like I might have to defend myself all over again, until Kiki stood up, and everyone got silent in about two seconds.

"You guys are so annoying," Kiki said, to her tablemates. "Leave Arnold alone. I'm going to sit over here with them." And she picked up her tray, walked over to my new table, and sat right between Evan and me.

"So, Arnold-slash-Ghostie, man of mystery," Kiki said, "is it too dangerous to be friends with you?"

I was relieved to finally be able to give someone a totally honest answer.

"I sure hope not," I said.

SARAH ANNE

The rest of the school day, I tried to mind my own business, and I thought I did a pretty good job. At the final bell, Evan and Kiki were waiting for me in the hall.

"I really don't want to answer any more questions about my parents," I told them.

Kiki laughed. "You're full of secrets, aren't you?"

Which was another question I didn't want to answer.

"Do you want to walk home with us?" Evan asked. "We both live pretty near the Kinders."

I looked up and down the hall.

"Are you looking for Ross and Brett?" Kiki asked, reading my mind.

"The kid with the backward hat and the kid with long hair and freckles?"

"Yeah, that's them." Kiki giggled. "They left already. I think they got a little spooked by your spy story."

"And that's exactly what it was, a story," Evan added. "A *made-up* story."

"I'm supposed to take the bus," I told them. "My cousin Lester is waiting for me."

Kiki rolled her eyes. "Lester who, Kinder? He's your cousin? He's in my brother's grade. No offense or anything, but he's kind of obnoxious."

"Lester wasn't happy when my aunt and uncle agreed to look after me," I told them. "But he's okay, I guess." My feelings about Lester were complicated. On the one hand, Kiki was right—he was pretty annoying. But on the other hand, my secret was in his hands. "Anyway, he should be here any second."

"I've never met him," Evan said.

Kiki giggled again—it turned out she was a giggler. "Lucky you."

Right on cue, Lester came around the corner, yakking loudly with two of his friends.

"ARNOLD!" he hollered. "If it isn't Arnold Z. Ombee, as I live and breathe!" He winked at me, I think because of the "breathe" reference. I pretended not to notice.

"What does the Z stand for, anyway?" asked Evan.

"Zip-a-dee-doo-dah!" Lester yelped, which seemed like as good an answer as any.

"Hey, Lester, you don't have to say my whole name, just Arnold is fine," I said.

"This is my cousin, Arnold Z. Ombee," Lester announced to his friends. "No cracks about his looks, he's got a lot of health issues. And besides, Darlene thinks he's super cute."

Lester's friends nodded at me like they couldn't care less. Lester smacked my backpack. "Everything go okay today?"

"Pretty good, I guess," I told him. "These are my classmates, Kiki and Evan."

"Oh yeah, I know Kiki—what's up?" Lester said. "What are you doing with Arnold?"

"Just hanging out," she said. "We're friends."

Lester looked confused. "Seriously? Why?"

Kiki shrugged. "Because interesting people interest me, I guess."

"Well, Arnold's interesting, that's for sure!" Lester turned his attention to Evan. "Yo, dude, what happened to your leg?"

Evan shifted uncomfortably. "I had cancer."

"Whoa, sorry to hear it, buddy," Lester said. He turned to Kiki. "You guys taking care of Arnold here? It's never easy, being the new kid."

"He's doing great," Kiki said. "We've got everything under control."

"Kind of," I added. "Some kids are nicer than others."

Lester's eyes flashed. "Well, you show me the kids who aren't nice, and I'll show you kids with two black eyes."

That surprised me. Lester gave me such a hard time at the Kinders' house, but I guess he decided maybe he'd look out for me at school. "You don't have to do that," I said, "but thanks."

"Listen, just because I think you're a little weirdo, doesn't mean other people are allowed to think so, too." Lester picked up his backpack. "You ready to grab the bus?"

"Actually, I'm going to walk home with these guys, if that's okay."

He frowned. "I don't know. Mom and Dad made me promise to get you home safe."

"I'll be fine, I swear."

"All right," Lester said. "Just don't die on me." Then he winked and cracked up.

"Ha-ha," I said. "You're hilarious."

We headed outside, where kids were piling on the buses. There was no sign of Ross or Brett, so I guess Kiki was right—they'd already moved on. But there was some kind of commotion going on, and I wasn't sure what it was until Kiki said, "Why is Sarah Anne sitting in the middle of the road?" I looked over and there she was, sitting by herself right in front of a school bus, clutching some sort of board in her hands. A bunch of adults were gathered around, trying to figure out what to do.

We walked over to where Mrs. Huggle was standing. "What's going on?" Kiki asked.

"Sarah Anne is having a bit of a tough time right now," Mrs. Huggle said. "Her mom's running a little late, and she left Henry inside."

"Henry?" I asked.

A few seconds later Ms. Frawley, the woman who was always with Sarah Anne, came out of the school carrying a small stuffed animal horse, who must have been Henry. Sarah Anne immediately got up, grabbed Henry, and hugged it tightly. Then she ran into Ms. Frawley's arms, burying her head in the woman's shoulder. Just like that, the crisis was over.

Kiki shook her head. "It must be hard to be so different from everyone else," she said.

I knew the feeling.

BECOMING FRIENDS

Walking home with Evan and Kiki, the world seemed to slow down and take a deep breath. I could relax with them. We didn't even have to talk. It wasn't weird, it wasn't stressful, and it wasn't scary.

It just was.

"Where do you guys live?" I asked, after we'd been walking for a few minutes.

Kiki pointed. "My house is up this road," she said. "Well, my mom and me. My dad lives a couple of towns over."

"Oh." I didn't know what that meant. I had figured all moms and dads lived together like Jenny and Bill.

"I live across the bridge from Clarendon Hill," Evan said.

A chill went up my already cold spine. That was where the Kinders had found me.

"I didn't realize humans lived there," I said, before realizing it.

"'Humans?'" Kiki said. "Yup, actual humans live there."

"It's a really nice neighborhood," added Evan, giggling. "For humans, and dogs and cats, too."

I decided I needed to change the subject quickly. "When did you have cancer?" I asked, instead of what I really wanted to know, which was *What exactly* is *cancer?*

"Whoa," Evan said, "where did that come from?"

"I don't know. You don't have to tell me if you don't want to."

Kiki kicked a rock.

"I got a really rare form of bone cancer when I was a baby," Evan said. "The doctors operated once, but when the cancer came back, they decided they had to amputate."

"I see," I said. "It seems very unusual to have only one leg, is that correct?"

Evan and Kiki looked at each other.

"What, are you from Mars?" Kiki said. "Yeah, that's correct."

"I'm sorry," I said. "I'm from a very small town, I haven't met that many people."

Evan shrugged. "It's fine. I'm used to it. Anyway, I can't

even remember what it was like to have two legs, so it's like normal for me."

"What's normal, anyway?" Kiki asked. "Is anyone really normal?" She twirled around five times really fast, like a spinning top. "I hope I'm never normal. Normal is overrated!"

I thought about that for a second. I wished I could tell them who I really was, so they'd know how normal they really were. But I couldn't.

"Normal is overrated," I repeated. "Got it."

We heard a loud *honk!* and turned around to see a big car pulling up alongside.

"Evan!" said a voice from inside the car. "Is that you?"

"Mom?" Evan said.

The car door opened and a woman with white-yellow hair on her head and a very upset look on her face got out. "Evan! Why are you walking home? Why didn't you take the bus? You know you shouldn't be walking all this way!"

Evan looked embarrassed. "I wanted to walk with these guys," he mumbled.

Evan's mom looked over at me and Kiki. "Hi, Kiki," she said. "You know this isn't good for Evan. That's what the bus is for. I'm surprised at you. You're usually so responsible."

"Sorry, Mrs. Brantley," Kiki said. "I wanted to walk home with our new friend, and Evan wanted to come along."

But Evan's mom wasn't paying attention to Kiki anymore—she was looking directly at me. "And who is this new friend?"

Uh-oh, I thought. *My first parent.*

The Kinders had warned me about parents.

"They can be a lot more brutal than the kids," they'd said.

I tried to look Evan's mother in the eye. "My name is Arnold," I said.

"Today was Arnold's first day," Evan explained. "Like Kiki said, that's one reason I wanted to walk, so we could all be together and get to know each other more."

Evan's mom looked me up and down, several times. "Well, hello, young man," she said. "Are you from around here?"

"I'm staying with my aunt and uncle, the Kinders," I said, dodging the question. "Do you know them?"

She nodded. "A little bit, yes."

There was a rustling noise from her car, and for the first time I noticed she had two dogs. One was very large, and the other was very small.

"Oh!" I said.

"Are you scared of dogs?" Evan asked. "They're really friendly."

I shook my head. "No. I mean, yes. I mean, a little I guess."

Evan pointed at the big one. "That's Lucy. She's a total sweetheart. You can pet her, if you want. But stay away from the little one, Spike. He's feisty."

I went to the car window and nervously scratched Lucy's giant head. It was furry and soft. "Hi there," I said. "Nice to meet you." Lucy gave out a loud happy groan, which caused

Spike to swing his snout around and yap noisily in my direction. I saw his large fangs and took a giant step backward.

Evan's mom laughed sharply. "Well, I think that's a sign we should be on our way, don't you? Arnold, it was lovely to meet you." She turned to Evan and her smile faded. "In the car, please. That's quite enough exercise for one day."

"But, Mom!" Evan moaned.

"No 'but, Mom,'" said Mrs. Brantley. "Let's go."

Without another word, Evan got in the car.

Mrs. Brantley nodded, and gave me one last long look. "Well, Arnold, welcome to our town. I hope you feel at home here."

Evan waved at us sadly as they drove away.

"She's really overprotective of Evan," Kiki said, as we kept walking. "I think that might be one reason why he doesn't have that many friends."

"I'll be his friend," I said.

And I meant it.

We walked and talked for about ten more minutes until Kiki dropped me off in front of my house.

"Thanks for being so nice to me on my first day," I told her.

"I wasn't being nice—I am nice," she said.

"Oh, right, sorry."

I stared at her, trying to figure out why a girl like her would want to be friends with a "boy" like me.

She punched me lightly on the shoulder. "Anyway, it's not every day we get someone new and interesting in our quiet little town," she said, answering my unasked question. "See you tomorrow."

HOME ALONE

When I walked through the front door, I was greeted by something very unusual.

Silence.

I realized that it was the first time I'd been totally alone in the house since the Kinders found me wandering in the road. Either Bill or Jenny had been with me, or near me, every second of every day. But neither of them was home, and Lester must have gone to a friend's house or something.

So I was by myself.

I wasn't sure what to do, at first. There was a bag of jelly beans on the kitchen table, with a note.

> Help yourself. Home around six. Can't wait to hear all about your day! Jenny.

I ate a few, then turned the TV on. Some show was on where somebody was talking to somebody else, with a whole bunch of people sitting in chairs watching them. Then the person who was doing most of the talking started to cry, and then somebody else came out to talk with the other two people, and then two of the three people got really mad at each other and started yelling, and some of the people watching in the chairs started yelling, too, and that's when I turned it off.

Then I went back into the kitchen and opened the refrigerator. There was a lot of human food in there. I took out an egg and stared at it. It looked like a giant white jelly bean. I tried to figure out how to open it, but I couldn't. I rolled it across the counter, which was kind of fun, for a minute. Then I rolled it a little bit too hard, and it fell onto the kitchen floor and cracked. Oozy, gooey, sticky liquid seeped out of the sides.

So that was how you opened it.

Then I walked into the bathroom. I turned the shower on and off, because I was still amazed that you could turn a knob and make water come out. The water was cold. And then I flushed the toilet, which was also amazing, because the water disappeared and then came back to the same exact place. After I flushed the toilet, I touched the shower water, and it was really hot. It was like magic! And then a few seconds later the shower water got cold again, so I flushed the toilet again to see if the water would get hot again, and it did. I couldn't figure out why that happened, even after I did it five more times. Then I looked down on the floor and noticed there was water all over the place, so I got a bunch of towels and soaked all the water up and then put them in the washing machine because I'd seen Bill and Jenny do that, even though I didn't understand that either, because why would you need to wash towels with water when they were already wet?

There was a lot about human life that just didn't make any sense.

Eventually, I went outside and waited for someone to get home, because I realized that being home alone wasn't very much fun, even in a nice warm house like the Kinders'.

That night at dinner, Bill and Jenny sat at the kitchen table, eating something they called chili, even though it was very hot. Lester was eating dinner in the TV room, which they let him do sometimes, especially if they wanted to talk to me without Lester interrupting an average of every thirty-eight seconds (I counted one night).

I was having jelly beans for dinner, in case you were wondering.

"Tell us about your first day," Jenny said.

"My first day ever?"

"Your first day at school," she clarified.

"Oh. Well, the bus ride was hard at first," I told them. "But then I met two really nice people, Kiki and Evan, who became my friends. Kiki said she wanted to be friends with me because I was new and interesting."

Bill and Jenny glanced at each other but didn't say anything.

"And my teacher, Mrs. Huggle, is nice, too. I raised my hand a lot at the beginning of the day, but then I realized people don't like other people who know all the answers. It's like when Lester told me to stop using words with four syllables or more."

Bill frowned. "He told you that?"

"Yes," I said, nodding. "He said young humans don't talk like that."

"He's right," said Jenny.

"And there were a couple of people who were a little mean to me, but I think that's also because I'm new and interesting," I went on. "Some people like it if you're new and interesting, but a lot of other people don't like it at all. At lunch people tried to ask me who I was and where I was from, but I didn't tell them. But then some people decided that the reason I was being secretive was because my parents were spies on a dangerous mission. And at first I was going to tell everyone how implausible that was, but then I decided not to."

"Implausible?" I heard Lester yell from the other room. "What did we say about that kind of language?"

Bill and Jenny looked shocked. I don't think they'd ever heard me say that many words in a row, in all the days I'd been there.

"Also, I saw Lester after school, and he offered to beat up the kids who were mean to me."

"You know it!" hollered Lester.

"Thank you for that report, Arnold," said Jenny. "Your first day sounds very . . . eventful."

"You're welcome."

"So what you're saying," said Bill, "is that the kids at school think your parents are international spies?"

"Not all. But most."

I waited for them to be mad because I had kind of sort of lied, but instead, both of them burst into laughter.

"Never underestimate the imaginations of fifth graders," said Jenny.

dodgEBALL

The next day was my first gym class.

I have to say, Bill and Jenny didn't adequately prepare me for what that meant.

It turned out that Ross, the backward hat kid, and Brett, the long-haired kid, were the best athletes in the class. I discovered that when the gym teacher, Coach Hank, said, "Ross! Brett! Choose up sides, you superstuds!"

"What does superstud mean?" I whispered to Evan.

"It means stay out of their way," he whispered back.

Earlier, I'd introduced myself to Coach Hank by giving him my doctor's note. He looked at me. "A skin condition *and* a leaky heart valve? Jeepers, kid, I'm sure not going to argue with this." He looked me over. "You look like death on a bad day, no offense. Nice to meet you, and sorry you're such a mess. My name's Hank, but you can call me Coach

Hank!" I guess he thought that was hilarious, because he practically doubled over with laughter. Then he stuck out his hand. I shook it, which was a big mistake. I think he broke all eight bones in my wrist.

"Ow," I said, which was a fib, because I don't feel pain.

I was starting to get the hang of this fibbing thing.

Coach Hank blew his whistle, which nearly split my eardrums in half. As the kids came running, he smacked me on the back. "You like dodgeball? We're gonna play a little dodgeball! No real running, so you should be fine. Besides, we have Field Day coming up this Sunday, so you have to practice!"

"What's Field Day?" I asked.

"Only the most fun day of the WHOLE YEAR!" roared Coach Hank. "Relay races, burgers, and dogs ... It's a BLAST!"

I glanced over at Evan, who rolled his eyes and shrugged. But I decided Coach Hank wasn't a guy you said no to.

"There's really no running in dodgeball?" I asked.

Coach Hank shook his head like his life depended on it. "Nope. No running. Just dodging."

I thought for a second. I'd already had enough trouble fitting in with the other students, now I was going to skip gym class, too?

You might as well have put a sign on my back that said TOTAL LOSER.

"Okay, I'll play I guess."

"Excellent!" Hank roared. "Ross! Brett! Choose up sides!"

Ross and Brett came jogging over, incredibly slowly.

"They don't look all that athletic to me," I whispered to Evan.

"That's how you run when you want to show everyone how cool you are," he explained.

"Ah, got it." I peered down at the other end of the gym, where girls' gym was going on. They were chatting, laughing, and throwing balls back and forth to one another.

To tell you the truth, that looked like a lot more fun.

"Okay, let's do this," Ross said. "I got Eric."

Eric, a kid who looked like he was about to burst out of his shirt, had a big smile on his face as he loped over to stand behind Ross. It was apparently a big honor to be picked first.

"Sammy, you're with me," Brett said, and a boy no bigger than me ambled over to Brett's side.

"He's short, but he's got a great arm," explained Evan.

Sammy and Brett held out their fists and knocked them into each other, which must have been some weird form of human handshake.

They started calling out names much faster.

"Simon."

"George."

"James."

"Kevin."

"Todd."

"Kyle."

And on it went, until there were only two boys left standing.

One was Evan.

I don't want to give away who the other one was, but his fake last name rhymes with *Schrombee*.

"I'll take Evan, I guess," Brett said, with a look on his face like he'd just smelled rotten milk.

And then there was one.

Yup. There I stood, in my long-sleeved shirt and baggy pants, with all the other boys in the grade staring back at me like I was some sort of alien.

Oh, wait. I *was* some sort of alien.

"Coach Hank?" called Ross. "Do we, uh, do we have to pick the new kid?"

"Yeah," agreed Brett. "The teams are even right now. We don't want it to be unfair or anything."

I stood there while the other boys snickered. As embarrassing as it was not to be picked, I would have been perfectly happy to sit this one out.

Alas, it was not to be.

"Forget it!" Coach Hank roared. "Arnold loves dodgeball! Get him in there!"

Ross rolled his eyes. "Fine," he mumbled. "Ombee, over here."

I could feel everyone's eyes on me as I walked over to stand with my teammates.

"Dude, where are your gym shorts?" asked one kid.

"He can't wear them because he's, like, got leukemia or something," another kid answered.

"What does leukemia have to do with wearing gym shorts?" a third kid asked.

I ignored them. Or pretended to.

"Game on!" Coach Hank bellowed. All the kids on my team ran to one wall, while Brett's team ran to the opposite wall. Coach Hank rolled out five balls per team, and kids started whipping them at one another as hard as they could.

Which is when I realized the object of the game was to tear somebody's face off with the ball.

"Do NOT throw at the head!" screamed Coach Hank. And then louder: "NOT AT THE HEAD!" But nobody was paying any attention to him.

It seemed like once instinct took over, there was no stopping a human on the hunt.

"Yo, Ghostie! Yo!" Evan yelled. He was crouching down near the opposite wall. "Do what I do! Go to the back and hide behind someone else! That way, they can't hit you!"

Less than a second later, a big red rubber ball crunched into his right shoulder.

"OWWW!" screeched Evan. He went to stand on the side-line, next to the other boys who'd already been bonked.

Balls kept flying back and forth, but amazingly enough, I was able to avoid each and every one. Remember I told you my arms and legs were really elastic? Well, combine that with the fact that I'm so pale and skinny that I'm practically see-through, and what you've got is a pretty good dodgeball player.

Well, good at dodging, anyway.

Not so good at throwing, as it turned out.

After a few more minutes, there were only a few players left on each team.

Then a ball rolled in my direction, and I picked it up.

"What are you waiting for, dork?" screamed Ross, my supportive captain. "Throw it, already! Nail someone!"

But I didn't *want* to nail someone. I wanted to go lie down and eat jelly beans. I don't have a violent bone in my body, I really don't, no matter what anyone says.

"THROW IT!" Ross screamed again.

Still, I hesitated. I should probably add here that I can't throw. It's hard to throw when your muscle mass is basically zero. So I gave the ball a little push, and it started rolling very, very slowly. Everyone stared at it, as if it had just sprouted legs and was walking its way across the gym floor.

"Are you kidding me right now?" Ross hollered. "That is, like, the most pathetic throw I've ever seen!"

"I'm sorry," I said, and I was about to make some excuse about how I'd just gotten my flu shot, so my arm was sore, when I saw Brett wind up and fire. I tried to yell, "Look out!" to Ross, but I can't yell very loud, and nobody heard me.

Sure enough, Ross got nailed right in the . . . well, it's above the legs and below the stomach, if you know what I mean.

Ross doubled over and made a noise that sounded like a combination of a horse sneezing and a pig giving birth. Then Ross's face turned a shade of purple I'd never seen before, and he keeled over onto the ground.

"Time out!" hollered Coach Hank. "TIME OUT!"

An eerie quiet fell over the gym as Coach Hank hurried to check on Ross. The poor kid couldn't talk, but he did manage to point at me with an accusatory finger.

"I think he's saying that it's Arnold's fault," Brett pointed out unhelpfully. "If he hadn't rolled the ball like a total doofus and gotten everyone so distracted, Ross would have seen my throw coming a mile away." Brett leaned over to where Ross was re-teaching himself how to breathe. "Sorry, buddy. Didn't mean to hit you, you know, down there."

Ross coughed and sputtered, then lifted himself to one knee. It took him about twenty seconds, but he finally managed to stare right at me and say a single sentence.

"I'll see you after school," he said.

sudoRls zomButam

"So then what happened?" asked Kiki.

I held the door open for her as we walked into our classroom. "Well, then Coach Hank said the rest of the dodgeball game was cancelled, and no one would be declared the winner. Of course, everyone blamed me for that, too, and so now I'm not just the weird new kid, I'm the weird new kid who ruined gym."

"Ouch," said Kiki, but she was humming to herself as she said it.

"Do you always have to be in such a good mood?" I asked her.

"Oh! Sorry, I'll stop." Five seconds later she was singing again.

We sat down at our desks. I noticed everyone looking at me, but they weren't curious if I was a spy anymore. They were mad. They were mad that I wasn't athletic, and they were mad that I looked strange, and they were

mad that I'd somehow caused the best athlete in the grade to be in a lot of pain.

But mostly, they were mad because I was different.

I looked over at Sarah Anne, the girl with the pink ribbon in her hair, who was sitting with Ms. Frawley, her helper. They were doing something with the board that Sarah Anne was always holding. She was different, too, but nobody seemed to bother her. The other kids just left her alone, maybe because they'd gotten used to her. She was lucky that way.

Maybe someday they'd get used to me, too.

Ross came in, limping and leaning on Brett. They headed straight for my desk.

"Uh-oh," said Evan. He slouched over and tried to make himself invisible.

Kiki gave me an encouraging smile. "Just ignore them," she suggested. "They're not worth it."

I glanced up at the front of the classroom, but Mrs. Huggle had walked over to talk to Ms. Frawley. Meanwhile, Ross was getting closer.

I stood up.

"What are you doing?" Kiki whispered urgently.

"If he's going to beat me up, I'd like to just get it over with." I was only halfway through my second day of school, and already I'd had enough. Who was I kidding, pretending I was a regular human? What a joke. I wasn't one of them, and I never *would be* one of them.

"Maybe I should just tell them who I really am," I said to myself. But apparently, I said it out loud, because Kiki and Evan both stared up at me.

"Who you really are?" repeated Evan. "Like, you mean you're actually from a family of spies? You can't tell them that. Won't you get arrested or something?"

"I'm pretty sure your parents aren't spies," Kiki said. "And neither are you, right, Arnold?"

I was trying to decide how to answer that, when I got distracted by something that was dropped on my desk with a big *plop!*

"Yo, Ombee, I think you left this in the gym," Brett said.

"It's your left shoe," added Ross, in case I couldn't see it for myself.

"That's correct," I said. "It is. Thank you very much for retrieving it." I guess my shoe had fallen off during all the dodgeball craziness, but I hadn't noticed. Probably because I'd never worn shoes before meeting the Kinders.

I reached out to put the shoe back on, but Ross's hand shot out and grabbed my arm. "Hold up. I need to ask you something first." He pointed at the shoe. "What's that?"

Everyone else in the class leaned in, except for Mrs. Huggle, Sarah Anne, and Ms. Frawley. It seemed pretty clear that the teacher wasn't going to bail me out. I was on my own.

"What's what?"

Brett pointed this time. *"That,"* he said, with a voice of pure disgust. *"Inside the shoe."*

We all looked. Sure enough, on the inner lining of the sneaker was a streak of a yellow, filmy liquid.

The technical term for it is *sudoris zombutam.*

Or, in language you might understand: zombie sweat.

So yes, as it turns out, zombies do sweat. Stress causes perspiration in zombies, just like in humans, and I guess I'd been stressed out in gym. When the Kinders first saw my zombie sweat, they pretended not to be grossed out, but I'm pretty sure they were. That was when they showed me this amazing thing called a washing machine, which fixed everything.

Unfortunately, there was no washing machine in the

classroom. So there it was, zombie sweat in my shoe, yellow, and sticky, and oozy.

I should also probably mention that it didn't smell very good. Especially to humans.

The entire classroom groaned with disgust. Mrs. Huggle looked up, confused. "Class? Class, what is it?"

Evan's eyes started to water. "Ewww, I need a drink," he said, hurrying to the sink in the back of the room.

Even Kiki, who was usually pretty tough, looked like she might throw up. "Um, Arnold, what is that? Are you okay?"

I tried to laugh it off. "Of course I'm okay! I told you about my condition, right? The one that makes it hard for me to run, and throw, and be active? This is part of it! It's one of the symptoms!"

But this time, I was pretty sure no one believed me. My luck had run out.

Telling people my parents were spies was one thing.

Trying to explain a thick yellow goo was another.

Ross leaned over my desk, wincing. (I guess his you-know-what still hurt.) "You need to tell us what's really going on here, Ombee," he said, in a scary whisper.

A random girl chimed in, "You're, like, the weirdest new kid ever."

Soon, the whole class was murmuring, talking about the strange-looking pale-skinned weirdo who had yellow ooze on his shoe.

"You guys don't know what you're talking about!" Kiki protested, trying to stick up for me—but no one was paying attention to her. One against twenty isn't exactly a fair fight.

Finally Ross shushed the crowd. "So, like I said earlier," he said, "I'll see you after school, by the jungle gym, and we'll settle this thing once and for all."

"Fine," I said, already trying to figure out an escape route back to the Kinders—a route that didn't go anywhere near the jungle gym.

"What's going on back there?" Mrs. Huggle was finally paying attention to what was happening in our little corner of the room. She started cutting through the desks to get back to where we were sitting, but unfortunately she stepped right into some of my sweaty, swampy ooze that had fallen onto the floor. She slipped and fell down flat on her back, with a big *fwwwwomp!*

The class sat there stunned for a second. "Are you okay?" murmured a few brave souls.

I was frozen in my seat. Ms. Frawley came running over and helped Mrs. Huggle up. She brushed herself off and looked down at the yellow muck that had caused her to fall. "What is that?"

"I have a condition that causes my secretions to be extra thick and full of mucus," I said.

Her nose wrinkled up in barely disguised discomfort. She hesitated while she tried to figure out what to say to that, before deciding on "I see. Well, I'm very sorry to hear that, and I hope you're okay. I will call the custodial staff to help clean this up."

I decided right then and there that Mrs. Huggle would be my favorite teacher for all time. "I hope you're okay, too," I said.

"I'm fine, thank you." She walked slowly to the front of the room. "Very well, then. It's time for snack."

A cheer went up as kids reached into their desks and brought out an assortment of baked good, salty treats, and—for the unfortunate few—raw vegetables.

"Snack?" I whispered to Evan. "What's that?"

"Whaddya mean, what's that?" He was already busy stuffing gluten-free, sugar-free cookies into his mouth. "It's only the best part of the day, that's what."

"Why didn't we have snack yesterday?"

Evan rolled his eyes like it was the most obvious answer in the world. "Because we had early lunch! Today we have late lunch."

"Oh. Right."

The next thing I knew, all the kids were sitting happily in their seats, chomping away.

Never underestimate the power of food.

PUddINg

There was about thirty seconds of people chewing, munching, and slurping before people started to notice I was just sitting there.

"Arnold?" Kiki was looking at me. "Don't you have a snack?"

Uh-oh. I guess the Kinders forgot about this part of the school day.

And I was all out of jelly beans.

"I left my snack at home," I said. "It's fine, though, I'm still full from breakfast."

Kiki held out something brown and creamy. "Here, you can have some of mine. It's chocolate pudding. Which happens to be the best food ever invented."

"Oh, no thanks."

She shrugged. "Suit yourself." Kiki took another spoonful. "Mmmmm. Yummy."

"Looks delicious," I said, even though it looked the opposite of delicious.

"The stuff those kids were saying to you before was so mean," Kiki said. "This whole class should be ashamed of itself. People can be so nasty sometimes."

"They're just being kids," I said, which may have been the truest thing I'd said all day.

Kiki turned to her right, where Brett was scarfing down some pretzels. "Hey, Brett," she said. "You guys can be real jerks sometimes, you know that?"

Brett stopped mid-chew. "Mind your own beeswax why don't you?" Then he looked at me. "Where's your snack? Oh wait, I forgot, you don't eat real food."

"What are you talking about?" Kiki asked.

Brett snorted. "Didn't you notice? Yesterday he didn't eat anything at lunch except jelly beans."

Kiki looked at me. "Is that true?"

"I have lots of allergies and a very small appetite," I said.

"So what else do you eat, then?" Brett asked. "Flowers? Dirt? Small insects?" He picked up a piece of paper and waved it in my face. "Maybe you eat homework. Do you eat homework?" He stood up so the whole class could hear him. "HEY, EVERYONE, THE NEW KID ATE MY HOMEWORK!"

"That's quite enough, Mr. Dorfman," said Mrs. Huggle. Brett sat down with a smug smile on his face.

Kiki shook her head in annoyance. "Don't let him bother you," she told me, "it's not worth it." Then she brought her chocolate pudding over to my desk. "Here, have a few bites. Come on, it's chocolate pudding! Who doesn't love chocolate pudding?"

Brett grinned. "Yeah, Arnold, who doesn't love chocolate pudding?"

"I don't," I said.

"Wow," said some girl in the second row. "Maybe he really is an alien."

Everyone laughed. Evan looked up from his cookies. Ross looked up from his whatever it was he was eating. And just like that, all eyes were on me.

Again.

I stared at the pudding. I knew I couldn't eat it. And yet.

"Thanks, Kiki, but I can't," I told her. "I— It's part of my condition—"

"EVERYTHING is part of your condition!" said Ross. "Eat it. Prove to us that you're at least a little bit human."

"Ross Klepsaw!" said Mrs. Huggle sharply. "That's enough."

He sat back, still staring at me.

"Come on," Kiki begged me. "If only to make them stop. Just one bite."

"Yeah, Arnold, go for it," added Evan. "Shut those guys up once and for all."

Kiki smiled her sweetest smile. "It won't kill you."

Well, I was pretty sure *that part* was true, at least.

I sighed. "Fine. One bite. Just for you guys." I picked up the spoon, dipped it in the pudding, lifted it to my lips, and took a tiny taste.

Remember I said that zombies don't sleep?

That's true.

But I never said zombies don't collapse.

KEEPING A SECRET

The next thing I remembered was opening my eyes and feeling a burning sensation that went clear through to the back of my skull.

I immediately knew why: Because zombies don't close their eyes. Why would we?

I also knew that I was still wearing the blue contact lenses the Kinders had made me wear, because they were stuck to my pupils.

"Is this it?" I said, to no one in particular. "Is it over?"

Suddenly, a woman in a white jacket was standing over me. "Is what over?" she asked.

I realized I was laying down. I also realized I was in a room I'd never been in before.

"Who am I?" I asked.

The woman frowned. "*Who* are you? You mean, where are you?"

"Oh, right," I said. "Where am I?"

"You're in the nurse's office, Arnold," she said. "I'm Nurse Raposo. Nice to meet you."

"Nice to meet you, too." I sat up. "My eyes feel really weird." I tried to act like I was in pain, because I knew a human would be. "Ow," I said. "Ow a lot."

"'Ow a lot?'" said Nurse Raposo. "I've never heard it put quite that way, but okay." She bent down to take a closer look. "What's going on in there? My goodness, your eyes are incredibly blue."

I quickly turned away. "What happened? Why am I in here?"

"Well, it appears you ate something that didn't agree with you," she said. "You took a bite of chocolate pudding, and down you went, completely unconscious."

"Wow," I said. "Yes, I'm allergic to certain foods."

"That might be the understatement of the year," said Nurse Raposo.

I closed my eyes again, just to see what it felt like. Also because I'd noticed that Nurse Raposo was still staring at me with a suspicious look in her eyes. But not the kind of suspicion that wanted to hurt me, like Ross or Brett. Hers was the kind of suspicion that seemed concerned—that wanted to help me.

"Do you want to tell me what's really going on?" she asked.

"What do you mean?"

"What do I mean?" The nurse pulled up a chair and sat next to me. "Well, I did some asking around and found out it's been quite an eventful first couple of days for you. You're incredibly bright, you're incredibly skinny, and you're incredibly pale. You refused to change for gym. You wouldn't throw a ball. You only ate jelly beans for lunch. You're wearing blue contact lenses, no matter what you say. And my guess is, you're wearing them to cover up a red streak across your eyes."

I tried to look at her but couldn't.

"So I'll ask again," she said. "Do you want to tell me what's going on?"

I did. I did want to tell her what was going on, really badly.

"I don't know what you're talking about," I said.

But she never took her eyes off me. "What's your real name?"

"Excuse me?"

She sat down next to me and talked very, very softly. "I have a lot of friends and contacts in the medical profession, some of whom work for the government. We're a very close-knit group. I know a little bit about what's going on. It's okay. You can talk to me. So I'll ask again: What's your name?"

And all of a sudden, I felt like a giant balloon that had been popped. All the air started to go out of me, as I slowly shrank down to nothing.

"Norbus Clacknozzle," I said, my voice barely above a whisper.

Nurse Raposo walked over to the door, closed it, then sat back down. "I see," she said. "Well, now we're getting somewhere."

"Are you going to turn me in? Are you going to send me back to the Territory?"

"Of course not. I'm a nurse, not a government agent. And I don't mind telling you, I'm not a fan of what they're doing up there." She brought over a warm towel and pressed it to my forehead. "As long as you're a student at this school, it's my job to take care of you."

"Thank you," I said.

"How did you wind up with the Kinders?"

"They found me up on Clarendon Hill," I told her. "There was a breach, six of us escaped, and I was the only one who wasn't recaptured."

"So it *is* true." She sat back and took a deep breath. "You must have been very frightened."

"I don't know enough to be frightened. I can't remember anything from before."

"They probably programmed you to be without a memory," said Nurse Raposo. "Less complicated that way."

I didn't know what she meant by *less complicated*, so instead I said, "The Kinders found me and now I live with them and they're telling everyone that I'm their nephew."

"Well, they were very brave to take you in," she said.

"Why?"

"Because it's dangerous. I'm sure the government is still looking for you. They don't like having any loose ends running around out there."

I didn't know what that meant either, but I understood the idea of the Kinders being in danger. "I don't want them to get hurt," I said. "They have been so nice to me."

The nurse sat down and took a deep breath. "We're not going to let that happen. For now, here's what we're going to do: Tomorrow, you must bring me a list of everything you can and cannot do, everything you can and cannot eat, okay?"

"Yes," I said. "Although the second list is going to be short. All I can eat are jelly beans."

"Hmmm," said the nurse. "I'd heard something about that, too. Jelly beans it is, then." She tilted my head upward. "Look up at the ceiling."

I did as I was told, and she put a few drops of liquid into each of my eyes. Just like that, the burning sensation was gone, and I felt human again.

Well, humanish.

"I'm going to have Mr. or Mrs. Kinder pick you up," said Nurse Raposo, a few minutes later. "You'll be fine by tomorrow. But please, answer me one thing before you leave."

"Okay," I said, "I'll try."

"Why did you pick the name Arnold Z. Ombee? That's a little on the nose, don't you think?"

I blinked a few times, just to make sure my eyes were really back to normal. They were.

"I guess—I guess I want to be who I really am," I told her. "Even when I can't."

A RIdE IN THE RI9HT dIRECTIoN

Ten minutes later Nurse Raposo told me, "Your ride's here."

I went outside to find Bill or Jenny, but they weren't there—instead, it was Lester, with his bicycle. He was standing next to the girl I'd met at the mall—the blue-haired girl who took my picture and told me I should be a model.

"Yo, Arnold," Lester said. "You remember Darlene, right?"

"Hi, Darlene," I said.

I noticed they were holding hands.

Good for Lester, I thought.

Darlene grinned at me, and the little gold thing in her nose sparkled in the sunshine.

"You okay, little man?" she said. "You look a little paler than last time, if that's even possible."

Lester smacked the top of my head, not lightly. "Yeah, you look terrible, even for you. What the heck happened?"

"I ate chocolate pudding, and I guess I'm allergic," I told him. "I collapsed and had to go to the nurse's office."

"Why'd you do that?"

"The other kids were pressuring me. They all think I'm really weird."

"Weird kids rule," said Darlene.

Lester snickered. "They totally do."

I'm pretty sure they kissed right then, but I can't be positive, because I was too busy making sure my eyes were staring at something—*anything*—that wasn't them.

Lester hopped on the bike. "Come on, dude, let's hit it, or else they're gonna make me go to geometry."

"Where's Aunt Jenny or Uncle Bill?" I asked him. It sure did feel odd saying that.

"Aunt Jenny or Uncle Bill? Oh, right, yeah . . . They're working, you know how it is," he said, even though I had no idea how it was. "The nurse couldn't get ahold of them, so she asked me to get you."

"Well, that was nice of you," I said.

"Of course Lester's going to help out his little cousin," said Darlene. "Who wouldn't?"

"Darn right!" Lester said, smiling like he was the nicest, most concerned human in the world. "Besides, this gave me a good excuse to get out of class, so here I am. Let's do this."

"Well, I gotta get to science," Darlene said. "See you guys later."

"Can't wait!" said Lester. He stared at Darlene as she walked away. Poor guy, he was really in deep.

I looked at the bike. "Where am I supposed to go?"

He patted the handlebars in front of him. "Right up here, pal. Safe and comfortable."

"Are you sure?"

"Of course I'm sure."

I hesitated. "It doesn't look safe, and it definitely doesn't look comfortable. And if you don't mind, I've already had a very difficult day."

Lester sighed, then glanced at me with something that actually looked a little bit like concern.

"Listen, Arnold. It's always hard for the new kid. And since you're a little, uh, *different*, it's going to be even harder for you. I know Mom and Dad told you that but you don't realize it until it's happening. You have to be tough and not let it get to you. Do you think you can do that?"

"I guess so."

"Good. Now let's go before someone realizes I don't have an extra helmet."

I hopped on the handlebars, and the next thing I knew we were whizzing out of the school parking lot and heading home. I have to admit, it was kind of fun feeling the wind smack my face as we zipped along the road.

"Is Darlene your girlfriend?" I asked Lester, as we were flying down the road.

"Workin' on it," he answered.

The work seemed to be going well, as far as I could tell.

When we got to the house, Jenny was just pulling into the driveway. She ran up and hugged me as I jumped off the handlebars.

"My goodness, I raced home as soon as I saw the message! Are you okay, Arnold?"

"He's fine," Lester said, before I could answer. "Some kids thought it would be funny to make him eat chocolate pudding."

"What?" Jenny looked as mad as I've ever seen her. "Well, I'm going to march right over to that school and make sure they—"

"Please don't," I said, interrupting her. "Thanks, but that will just make it worse." I looked at Lester, then back at Jenny. "It's always hard for the new kid, especially someone like me. I just have to be tough. But I'll be fine. I promise."

"And I'm keeping an eye on things, too," Lester added, "just to make sure everything is okay."

I nodded at Lester. He nodded back. It seemed like maybe he wasn't going to always hate me after all.

It's amazing what one kiss can do.

A HARd CoNVERSATIoN

Getting ready for bed is not really much of a thing for me. I brush my teeth, which still feels really weird, and wash my face with warm water, which feels even weirder, and then I get under the covers and lay my head back on my pillow, which feels nice and soft.

The whole thing takes about two minutes.

Lester does a bunch of other stuff. He's really fascinated by his face for some reason, because he stares at it in the mirror for a long time before he goes to bed, and then he stares at it again for a long time the next morning, as if he expects it to change completely while he's sleeping. And he washes his hair at night, which gets out the stuff that he puts in his hair in the morning, which doesn't make sense, since if he didn't want it, he shouldn't have put it in his hair in the first place.

And humans think *zombies* are scary?

I was laying in bed when Bill and Jenny came in to my room.

"Hi," I said.

Neither one of them spoke for about thirty seconds. Then Jenny said, "We know how difficult this must be for you."

"I'm doing fine," I said. "Please don't worry. The nurse at school was very nice and helpful." For some reason I couldn't bring myself to tell them that Nurse Raposo knew who I really was. Maybe because I thought it would worry them. Or maybe because I thought they would think I'd let them down.

"We're very proud of you and so impressed by how well you're adjusting," said Jenny, softly. "We wanted you to know that."

Bill sat down on the edge of the bed. "Arnold, we haven't really asked about where you're from," he said. "Or whom you left behind. Do you want to talk about any of that? Because if you do, we'd like to talk about it, too."

I waited a few seconds before answering.

"I wish I could," I said. "But like I've said, I don't remember very much at all. I know there was a big room. And a big area they called a pen. And a tall fence. And I remember being told that humans were dangerous. Humans wanted to hurt us. Humans were the enemy."

Lester started playing music loudly in the next room. Jenny shut the door.

"We're not the enemy," Jenny said softly. "I hope you know that now."

"*You're* not the enemy," I told her. "But I'm not so sure about some of the other humans."

Bill scratched his head. "Maybe we should tell a few more people what's happening here. We need to be able to give Arnold some more support."

"No!" Jenny said, speaking as forcefully as I've ever heard her speak. "Not yet, it's still too risky. For Arnold, and for us."

Now it was Bill's turn to speak forcefully. "Well, I don't know how we're supposed to just indefinitely harbor an illegal, secret government zombie without some help. It's too much. We need a plan."

"I know," said Jenny. "I just need time to figure out what the plan is."

"Well, we should have thought about that before," said Bill.

Everything was quiet for a minute. I'd never heard them argue. I didn't like it one bit. And it was all because of me.

And then I remembered what Nurse Raposo said, about how brave Jenny and Bill were, and how dangerous it was.

"This is all my fault," I said. "Maybe Lester was right. Maybe I don't belong here."

"Of *course* you don't belong here!" Bill said. "To be honest, Arnold, I'm not sure you belong anywhere. But you're part of our family now, and that's all there is to it."

"Bill is right," said Jenny. "Now let's forget all about this, and just try to get some sleep."

"Or not," I said, and then we all did something that we hadn't ever done together.

We laughed.

March 5, 2027
GT 278
PROJECT Z
THE OUTER BRANCH
ARIZONA

ATTENTION ALL UNITS: There has been a possible
sighting of our missing subject.

A report came in through a branch in Clarendon
that a young child has recently matriculated
at an elementary school there. This young
child has suspicious traits that generated an
anonymous phone call to our central office.

Please bear in mind that this escape has been
kept CONFIDENTIAL from the general public, so
this tip must have come from an inside source,
or someone with knowledge of the project.

Regional command is leading the investigation
in order to ascertain more information and the
validity of this lead.

More information will be shared as it becomes
available.

Horace Brantley
Regional Commander, National Martial Services

RECESS

According to one of the Kinders' books I've read—the *Merriam-Webster Dictionary*—"recess" means *the temporary suspension of an activity or process*. But in elementary school, it apparently means run around like a crazy person for absolutely no reason.

The teachers and all the other adults at school must think recess is a productive use of time, however, because they schedule one every day. And they may be right. It turns out that if you let human children run around like lunatics for thirty-five minutes once a day, they are able to act like normal people the rest of the time.

😢 😎 😄

The first two days, I spent recess inside, because of my "sensitivity to the sun." I would read quietly at my desk, while different teachers took turns keeping an eye on me—which really meant doing stuff on their phones.

But the third day of school was cloudy.

"Why don't you come outside with the rest of the class today, Arnold?" Mrs. Huggle asked me, as the bell rang. "There's not too much sun to worry about, and you might enjoy getting some fresh air."

I glanced around—all the other kids were already piling out the door, choosing sides for whatever games they planned on playing.

"I don't know," I said. "I'm not really supposed to run around that much."

Kiki, who was eavesdropping as usual, butted in. "Aw, come on Arnold! You can come outside and do nothing if you want, lots of kids do. Do you really want Ross and Brett making fun of you for being such a weenie, especially after you fainted yesterday?"

"Okay, fine." I got my jacket—even though no one else was wearing one—and headed outside. There was a big field, where kids were chasing one another around in circles and then knocking each other over. There was the jungle gym that Ross had referred to the day before, which was some kind of structure that kids could climb on. And there was a cement rectangle with two big poles at either end, which was being used for a game that seemed to involve throwing orange balls into round circles with nets on them.

I took a deep breath and tried to decide what to do. My two friends, Kiki and Evan, were with a bunch of other kids playing tug of war in a sand pit. Pretty much everyone else was running around, too. There was only one person, a girl, who wasn't involved in some sort of game. She was sitting by herself on a bench near the playground, staring at something in her hands. A woman was sitting next to her, reading.

Staring and reading—those were two activities I was good at!

I decided to join them.

I was about halfway there when I realized the girl was Sarah Anne. I also saw that the thing she was holding was the board she always has. The woman with her was Ms. Frawley, who was always by her side. I hesitated, because I didn't want to disturb them. But before I could walk away, Ms. Frawley looked up and spotted me.

"Hello," she said. "Would you like to join us?"

Sarah Anne looked up, almost at me but not quite—it felt like she was looking at my right shoulder. Her eyes were a piercing green, and as she stared without blinking, I couldn't tell if she wanted me to sit down or get lost. Maybe it was neither. Then she looked back down at her board.

"Okay, sure," I said, and I sat down on the bench. "My name is Arnold. I'm new."

"Oh, I know," said Ms. Frawley. "My name is Ms. Frawley, and this is Sarah Anne. Are you enjoying school so far?"

"Yes, it's been great," I said. "Everyone is really nice."

Sarah Anne immediately picked up her board, which is when I noticed it had letters on it. I realized that she pointed at the letters to spell words, which was how she communicated. She pointed at two.

"HA," said Ms. Frawley, speaking for Sarah Anne.

I smiled. "Okay, well, I guess not *everybody* is really nice. But most people are."

Sarah Anne looked up at the sky, then back down at her board. Ms. Frawley watched her point at the letters.

"DO . . . YOU . . . LIKE . . . HORSES?" said Ms. Frawley.

"Sure," I said. "Horses are beautiful."

Sarah Anne pointed at her board.

"I . . . LOVE . . . HORSES," said Ms. Frawley.

I smiled. "That's great."

"WHERE . . . ARE . . . YOU . . . FROM?"

"Pretty far away," I said. "I doubt you would have ever heard of it. Have you lived here all your life?"

Sarah Anne pointed at her board, and Ms. Frawley spoke.

"YES . . . BUT . . . I . . . HOPE . . . TO . . . MOVE . . . TO . . . THE . . . CITY . . . WHEN . . . I . . . GROW . . . UP."

"To do what?" I asked.

"WORK . . . WITH . . . HORSES . . . AND . . . BECOME . . . A . . . POET."

Sarah Anne put her board down.

"You should see some of her poetry," said Ms. Frawley. "It's beautiful."

"I would love to," I said.

Sarah Anne looked at my shoulder for a long time, then picked up her board.

"MAYBE . . . SOMEDAY . . . I . . . WILL . . . SHOW . . . IT . . . TO . . . YOU."

She stopped, then thought of something else she wanted to say.

"IF . . . YOU'RE . . . LUCKY."

We didn't talk for the rest of the recess. We just watched the other kids run around. Sometimes Sarah Anne would make words on her board, and then Ms. Frawley would write them down on a piece of paper. Maybe it was a poem, but I didn't ask to see it. She'd show it to me if she wanted to.

When the bell rang, I got up.

"It was really nice to meet you, Sarah Anne," I said. "You, too, Ms. Frawley."

"We'll see you inside," said. Ms. Frawley.

Sarah Anne picked up her board and started pointing. As always, Ms. Frawley spoke the words that Sarah Anne was saying.

"DON'T . . . EAT . . . ANY . . . PUDDING . . . TODAY."

PAYBACK

I took Sarah Anne's advice and didn't eat any pudding at snack. I also didn't talk about my parents being spies at lunch, didn't play dodgeball at gym, and didn't produce any zombie sweat at all. In other words, I stayed as invisible as possible. Which, it turns out, isn't that hard to do when you're half-invisible already.

After school, Kiki and I decided to walk home together again, but Kiki couldn't leave right away, because she had to go to the office to sign up for soccer. "It will only take about fifteen minutes, but I can meet you after that, if you want to wait," she said.

After thinking about it for approximately zero seconds, I said, "Sure."

"You know, Arnold," she said to me, "you should join a sport, too. It's a great way to meet people."

"Maybe," I said. As in, *maybe never in a million years*.

As I headed down the hall to wait near the front door,

I felt a hand on my shoulder. It wasn't as warm as Bill's or Jenny's hands.

I turned around to see Ross standing there in his backward hat. His friend Brett was with him, his long hair covering half his freckly face.

"Did you think I forgot?" Ross asked.

"I don't know what you're talking about," I said, even though I knew exactly what he was talking about.

"Ha-ha, very funny." Ross looked down the hallway. "We had a date yesterday after school, but then you got sick from chocolate pudding."

"Who *does* that?" Brett asked. "Who gets sick from chocolate pudding?"

I looked around for someone—anyone—who might be walking down the hall, but there was no one there. It was like someone called a meeting of the whole school, and everyone was invited except Ross, Brett, and me.

"I don't want to fight you, Ross. I just want to go home."

I tried to walk around him, but he blocked my way. "Let me get this straight," he said. "You get to injure me in dodgeball, but I don't get to do anything back? How is that fair?"

"That was an accident, and you know it."

"All I know is, we have unfinished business, and it's time to finish it."

We stood there for a few seconds, staring at each other, while a bunch of other kids materialized out of nowhere. There must have been some sort of unspoken signal that was only audible to people under twelve years old.

"Are you guys gonna fight?" asked one kid, hopefully.

"If so, you better hurry up," said another. "The buses are leaving in five minutes."

The kids started murmuring, "Fight! Fight! Fight!"

I felt zombie sweat pooling in my shoes.

Humans are the enemy.

Humans will hurt you.

If you see a human, attack.

But my first instinct was not to attack, it was to yell. "Help! Help!" I croaked, before remembering I have a very soft voice.

Which brought me to my second instinct: run. But then I remembered I'm a terrible runner. My legs are like rubber.

My third instinct was realizing I was all out of instincts.

Ross pushed me up against a locker.

"Not such a tough guy now, are you?" he sneered.

"I never said I was a tough guy."

"Yeah, well . . ." Ross glared at me like he was trying to decide whether to punch me or laugh at me.

"Hit him!" urged Brett. "What are you waiting for?"

"He's just so . . . scrawny," Ross said. "It almost doesn't seem fair."

"I agree!" I said.

Ross pulled his hand back and made a fist. I braced myself for the punch, knowing it was likely that he was going to break my skin. Which wouldn't mean blood, of course. It might even mean more zombie sweat. I wasn't sure how I was going to explain *that* one.

Suddenly new words started ringing in my head.

If a human attacks you, immediately employ the zombie zing.

If a human attacks you, immediately employ the zombie zing.

And a fourth instinct formed in my head. The next thing I knew, for reasons I didn't even understand, I reached out with my right arm and pinched Ross on his left shoulder.

"Hey!" Ross looked at me, then looked at his left shoulder, then looked back at me. "What the—?"

And then he froze in place.

"Ross?" I said. "Ross? Ross, are you okay?"

But Ross couldn't speak, because he couldn't move.

Brett saw what was going on, and his eyes went wide. "Ross! Dude! Like, what are you doing? Are you okay?"

Ross's eyes darted back and forth—at least he could move them, which was a good sign.

We all stood there for a few seconds, almost as frozen as Ross was, waiting for him to move. But he didn't. As a confused murmur of panic rose up in the kids that had gathered around, I heard a voice coming from down the hall. "What the heck is going on here?" It was a voice I recognized, and I sighed with relief. Yep, there was Kiki, marching down the hallway, with Evan a few steps behind her.

"Ross! Are you about to beat up poor Arnold Z. Ombee? The skinniest kid in the whole class? Have you no decency?"

"Arnold pinched Ross on the shoulder, and now Ross can't move!" said Brett, breathlessly.

"HA!" said Kiki.

"It's true," I mumbled.

Kiki ran up to Ross. "Jeepers," she whispered. "Ross! Are you okay?"

Ross tried to speak, but it came out more like, "Mrfwhsrgork."

"Holy smokes," said Evan.

All the kids stared at me.

"What kind of a monster are you?" said Brett. "Is this some super spy trick? Are you some kind of freak?"

"I-I'm sorry," I stammered. "Ross was about to punch me in the face. I had to do something."

Humans are the enemy. Humans will hurt you. If you see a human, attack.

"Yeah, like defend yourself," Evan said. "Not paralyze the poor kid."

"I didn't mean to . . . I don't know . . . maybe I pinched a nerve in his neck."

"WELL, UNPINCH IT!" hollered Kiki. "Or else you're going to be in a ton of trouble!"

I could hear voices coming down the hall. Adult ones. This was it. I had to do something, and fast.

I reached out, put my hand on Ross's shoulder right where I'd pinched him, and pinched again.

And just like that, he was fine.

He shook his head like he'd just woken up from a nap. "What happened?" he asked groggily. "What are we doing in the hall?"

"You were just about to punch me in the face," I said. "I'm sorry, I didn't know what else to do."

Ross and Brett and all the other kids looked at me like I had just become the most powerful person on earth. Or at least, the most powerful person at Bernard J. Frumpstein Elementary School.

"Who are you?" whispered Ross.

Luckily I didn't have to answer that one, because right

then a teacher walked up. "What's this all about?" she said. "Why are you kids gathered in the hallway? You know you're supposed to be in lineup. The buses leave in three minutes. Get going!"

As the kids started to disperse, Kiki shook her head. "Wow, I leave you alone for ten minutes and this is what happens?"

"That was very odd," I said. "I swear, I'm as shocked as everyone else."

She laughed. "So then, you're not a space alien?"

"Of course not," I said, which was technically the truth. "Ross just had some really weird reaction, that's all."

"If you say so," Kiki said.

I glanced at Evan. He looked like he was having a harder time accepting my explanation than Kiki, but he decided not to say anything about it.

"Thanks for believing me," I said. "I really appreciate it."

"No problem," Kiki said. "That's what friends are for, right?"

"Right," I said, even though I actually had no idea what friends were for.

Because I'd never had one before.

A KNOCK ON THE dOOR

After all the excitement had died down, Kiki asked Evan if he wanted to walk home with us, but he shook his head. "My mom was really mad at me the other day," he said. "Ever since I got sick, she's been nervous about me doing too much and hurting myself and stuff like that."

"I understand," I said.

"I don't," Kiki said. "She has to let you live your life."

Evan smiled sadly and walked to the bus.

On the walk home, Kiki was nice enough to not talk about what happened with Ross anymore. Instead she asked me all sorts of questions about all sorts of stuff, like music (I told her I didn't listen to it very much), movies (I told her I hadn't seen very many), and what I wanted to be when we grew up (she said she wanted to be an emergency medical technician—whatever that was—and I told her I didn't know yet.)

"Jeez," she said, as we approached the Kinders' driveway.

"For a smart guy, you don't know anything about anything, do you?"

"I guess not."

Kiki looked at me like she was trying to decide something. "Well, that just means I get to tell you what to do and what to like, which is a good thing, right?"

"I guess so."

"Ha! You're a funny one, Arnold Z. Ombee." Then she punched my arm and went skipping away.

I walked up the driveway, wondering why Kiki thought I was funny since I couldn't remember ever making a joke in front of her.

I had just about recovered from the Zombie Zing episode and was feeling better when I went into the house—but as soon as I saw Jenny and Bill, I knew something was wrong. First of all, they were both there, and they were usually still working when I come home. Second of all, Bill didn't smile when he saw me. That had never ever happened before.

I pretended not to notice, though. Maybe if I didn't notice, it wouldn't be true.

"Today I met this really interesting girl named Sarah Anne," I told them. "She talks by pointing at letters on a—"

"People are talking about you," Jenny said.

I froze.

With those five words, I felt everything ending.

I looked at Bill. "I overheard a conversation down at the grocery store," he explained. "Apparently there's lots of scuttlebutt about a strange new boy in town. Rumors are flying."

I could feel my skin jumping off my bones. "Was it the nurse? She swore she wouldn't tell!"

"You told the nurse?" Jenny said, with a little quiver in her voice.

"She guessed! But she was really nice about it!"

Bill sighed heavily. "Well, maybe it was her. We don't know who is starting these rumors, and what exactly they're saying about you."

I couldn't believe it. The idea that the nurse would betray me didn't seem possible. She swore that she would keep my secret, and I had believed her.

"What do we do? Do I have to leave?"

"Of course not," Bill said. "Nobody has any proof about anything. And there are laws in place that prevent people from just doing what they want without proof. But it's clear you're going to be watched very carefully."

I was still trying to absorb this news when Jenny said, "There's something else."

I stared into space, waiting for her to speak.

"I ran into Mrs. Dorfman at the bank. She was asking about you."

"Who?" I asked

"Carol Dorfman. I guess she has a son that goes to school with you," she said. "Brett Dorfman?"

"Ugh," I said.

"Ugh what??!" came Lester's voice from the hallway. Two seconds later, he came lumbering into the kitchen. He took one look at us and his eyes went wide. "Whoa, you guys look like you just saw a zombie."

"Ha-ha," I said quietly.

Jenny looked at her son. "Lester, I'm sorry, but I have to ask: Did you say anything to anyone about who Arnold is?"

Lester looked mortally wounded. "Are you serious right now? Of course not!" He looked at me. "I've been watching out for him. Tell them, Arnold!"

I nodded. "It's true. Lester got really mad when I told him some kids were giving me a hard time. He threatened to beat them up."

"I sure did," Lester said, his head bobbing up and down. "No one messes with anyone in my family. Even if they're not actually in my family." Then his eyes narrowed. "Why? Did someone spill the beans on Arnold?"

Before either Bill or Jenny could answer, there was a knock on the door.

"Who could that be?" wondered Jenny aloud. They didn't have very many visitors, as far as I could tell.

After a few seconds, Bill got up. "I'll see what's going on," he said. "I'm sure it's nothing. Maybe the mailman with a package."

We all followed him as he went into the hallway. He opened the door, and two police officers were standing there, a man and a woman.

"Mr. Kinder?" said the policeman. "Mr. William Kinder?"

"That's right. What can I do for you?"

The two officers looked at each other, then back at Bill. "We're doing some canvassing in the area," said the policewoman, "and we'd like to ask you a question or two."

Bill touched his mustache. "What kind of questions?"

"Well, sir," said the policeman, "there was a little trouble over on Clarendon Hill a few weeks back, and we're just following up to make sure everything's gotten back to normal."

"What kind of trouble?"

"Unfortunately we're not at liberty to say just now."

Bill scratched his head, as if he had absolutely no idea what the policeman was talking about. "Well, everything's totally normal around here, that's for sure."

"Terrific," the policewoman said. "Do you mind if we take a look around your house for a quick minute?"

Bill smiled his broad, warm smile. "As long as you have a search warrant. Do you?"

The officers peered at Bill. "We do not, sir," said the woman.

"Well then, be sure to come back when you do," Bill said. He smiled again. "But I sure am glad to see the force is on the case."

The policeman narrowed his eyes, as if he were trying to decide if Bill was being serious or sarcastic. "Thank you, sir," he said.

"We were just about to sit down to a late lunch," Jenny said to the police officers. "Would either of you care for a glass of lemonade?"

"Oh, no, ma'am," said the policewoman. "We're on duty, and we've got to get back to it." She held out a card. "If either of you notices anything unusual, would you be so kind as to text us or give a call down at the station? Number's right there on the front."

Bill took the card. "We most certainly will. Good day, now."

He was about to close the door when the policeman held his hand up.

"Oh, one last thing. The neighbor mentioned you have a nephew staying with you, recently moved in?"

For the first time, I saw a nervous look cross Bill's face.

"That's right. My sister Betty's boy."

"Do you mind if I ask why you're looking after him?"

"Oh, she and her husband had to leave the country for a spell, and it seemed too much disruption for the boy to go along. It's just for six months or so. Why do you ask?"

"Oh, no reason." The policeman put his hand to his cap. "Thanks so much for your time. Have a good day, now."

After they left, we all walked slowly back to the kitchen.

Lester was the first to speak. "Now what?"

Jenny took a deep breath. "Well, we don't have a lot of time to figure out our next move, that's for sure," she said. "I have a sister in Connecticut who could come in handy."

"We'll have to talk about that," Bill said, exchanging a look with wife.

"Indeed," she said. Then Jenny looked at me. "For now, we keep living our lives," she said. "That's all we can do."

Technically I didn't have a life to live.

But I knew what she meant.

A PLAN

The first thing I heard the next morning was Lester letting out a howl.

"NO WAY!"

He came charging into the kitchen, where we were all having breakfast. "I didn't make the JV basketball team!" he said, panting with anger. "They just posted the team online. I was, like, the best one in the tryout! But I didn't make it!"

Bill looked up from his eggs. "Well, obviously there was some kind of mistake."

"I should say so," agreed Jenny. "We'll talk to the coach and find out what happened."

"No!" wailed Lester. "You can't do that! The coach is Tommy Klepsaw's dad! Tommy's younger brother is Ross! That's the kid who got nailed during the dodgeball game because of Arnold!"

Not to mention temporarily paralyzed by my Zombie Zing, I thought, but I wasn't about to bring that up.

Lester pointed an accusatory finger in my direction. "It's all your fault."

"Slow down," said Jenny. "What's all this about a dodge-ball game? Arnold, you played in a dodgeball game at school?"

"Kind of," I said, keeping my eyes on my jelly beans. "Two days ago. It was a mistake, I shouldn't have. I'm sorry."

Lester sat down with a pout. "It's not just that. I've tried to be nice and everything, but the truth is that Arnold is messing things up for me. All week at school my friends' little brothers and sisters have been texting them about my weird-looking cousin, and everyone's making fun of me for being related to him. And now people are going to find out that the police were here, and what am I supposed to say about that?"

Jenny and Bill looked at each other, but neither one said anything.

"What about Darlene?" I asked.

Lester snorted. "She's cool, but you know, she told me last night she's too busy to have a boyfriend right now."

"Oh," I said. "That's too bad."

"Yeah, it IS too bad." Lester drank a glass of orange juice in one gulp, which seemed to calm him down a little. "Listen, I get it. You're actually a decent kid, and I know how hard this must be for you. You're a zombie, for crying out loud! Trying to go to a human school! Who does that?" He let out a burp. "Excuse me. Anyway, I'm tired of feeling like the bad guy here, just because I think it's weird that we have a zombie living in our house who's pretending to be normal. It's not fair."

"Life isn't always about what's fair," Bill said quietly. "Arnold can tell you that."

"People are out there looking for him!" wailed Lester. "Someone is going to find out he escaped! We might all end up in jail, on top of everything else!"

"Lester's right," I said. "The last thing I want is to get you all in trouble."

"Nonsense," Bill said, standing up. "You're a child. A child who's different than us, who's from another place, another world even, but a child nonetheless. It's clearer to me than ever that the people who are trying to find you do not have your best interests at heart. So we are going to take care of you, because that is our job as compassionate people."

Lester stood up, too. "Whatever. I'm going to school. When I come home tonight, we better have a plan on how to deal with this."

But I was already thinking about a plan. A plan that would solve everything, and keep the Kinders safe.

I was going to go to school.

And then after school, I was going to leave.

Forever.

AN INVITATION

When I got to school, I noticed everyone was treating me differently. Meaning, differently from the earlier ways they'd been treating me differently.

Before, they'd looked at me like I was the weirdest kid on earth.

Now, thanks to the Zombie Zing, they looked at me like I was the most powerful kid on earth.

Everyone said hi to me, but kept their eyes down, like I was their boss or something. Brett nodded at me, gave a nervous smile, and didn't say anything. Ross just eyed me warily.

"How's your shoulder?" I asked him.

"Fine," he said. "Thank you."

"I'm glad."

Evan, who watched this exchange, looked very pleased to be friends with the newest tough guy in town. He had a big smile waiting for me when I sat down at my desk.

"Did you get my invitation?"

"Huh? What invitation?"

He leaned in as if to tell me the biggest secret ever. "To my party." He pointed at my desk. "In there."

I opened my desk drawer and found a piece of paper folded about a million times. "Wow," I said. "This looks like serious business."

"You can't be too careful," Evan said.

I unfolded it and read Evan's lousy handwriting.

LET'S CELEBRATE!
EVAN IS TURNING 11 AND YOU'RE INVITED!

"A birthday party?"

"More of a gathering," Evan said. Then he leaned over and flicked the back of my neck, for old times' sake. "It's Saturday night, and it's going to be so fun!"

"*This* Saturday night? In two days? Gosh, Evan, I had no idea it was your birthday."

"Well, I don't have that many friends to talk about it with, I guess." He smiled brightly. "But the party was my mom's idea, and she said I could invite you! You'll be there, right?"

I wasn't sure what to say. Based on the plan I'd made about thirty minutes earlier, I might be gone by then.

"Well, I—"

"It's a very exclusive gathering," Evan said. "I'm only inviting two people altogether—you and Kiki."

"Really? Why just us?" But as soon as I'd asked, I wished I hadn't. Because the answer was obvious. We were his only friends.

"It's a slumber party," Evan explained. When I looked at him blankly, he added, "A sleepover."

"Ah." Well, that clinched it. I would have to leave town before the party, because I couldn't possibly go to a sleepover. I don't sleep, remember? That could get awkward. And dangerous.

"I'd really love it if you could come," Evan said. "I really would. Really."

Uh-oh.

"I only invited two friends," Evan repeated, in case I hadn't absorbed that information the first time. He looked like he might dissolve into a small puddle if I said no.

Double uh-oh.

"I'll be there," I said, thinking that I'd need to practice being asleep, and fast.

"Great!" Evan exclaimed. "We're having chocolate pie!"

"Sounds delicious," I said.

So I'd run away Sunday, after the party.

I mean, it's not like anything crazy could happen, right?

Wrong.

dETECTIVE WORK

My goal for the next two days was to stay calm and avoid drama. I'd started to notice that Bill and Jenny were spending a lot of time talking quietly to each other, probably discussing what to do with me, but every time I asked, they'd smile and change the subject. Neither of them had heard any more information about a strange boy in town, so I think they were starting to convince themselves that everything would turn out fine.

I knew better. Somehow, I knew better.

At morning snack on Thursday, I made a point of taking out my jelly beans after everyone was already fully concentrating on their own treats. But that didn't stop Evan from noticing.

"How many jelly beans can one person eat?" he asked.

I pointed at his snack. "What's that, some sort of nuclear accident?"

Evan looked wounded. "This is my mom's special muffin recipe," he said.

 160

"Oh, sorry," I said. "I didn't know she made it."

"She's a great cook!" He peered down at his snack sadly. "But these muffins have no flour and no gluten, whatever gluten is. My mom says I need to eat healthy."

"Eating healthy is overrated," Ross said, eavesdropping. "And so is listening to you yap about your food."

"Mind your own business," Evan mumbled, "or Arnold will zing you again."

Ross was stunned. "You stink" was all he could come up with, before Mrs. Huggle said, "That's enough, boys."

I glanced over at Evan. He grinned back at me.

Boy, things had sure changed.

😫 😎 😋

Later, at lunch, I decided to try and figure out who had started the rumors about me. As far as I could tell, the only possible suspects were Nurse Raposo, who I'd pretty much ruled out, and I guess Coach Hank, who may have been tipped off by my pathetic dodgeball skills. But there are a lot of lousy athletes out there, right? And he didn't seem like the type—as far as I could tell, all he cared about was winning, losing, and yelling.

I was standing in the cafeteria, holding another tray of food that I wasn't going to eat and container of milk that I wasn't going to drink, when I saw Kiki at her usual table. I walked over, and a bunch of kids immediately scattered to make room for me.

"Thanks," I said, sitting down. I turned to Kiki. "Hey, can I ask you something?"

"Hold on a second." She was in the middle of telling a story to two girls and a boy, whose names I didn't know. Kiki had a lot of friends.

She got to the punch line—"And that's when he said to me, 'When's the last time you saw someone put strawberries inside a clarinet?' "—and the three others cracked up. After basking in the laughter for a few seconds, Kiki looked at me. "What's up?"

"What are you eating?"

"Oh, this?" She waved the food around. "It's a fish stick. You want a bite?"

"I'm allergic."

"What aren't you allergic to?"

"Yeah, I know." I leaned in. "So anyway, what I wanted to ask you is kind of private."

"Oh, okay," she said. "Let's go over here." We got up and walked over to the water fountain, which nobody ever used, because for some reason everyone seemed to prefer buying water in a bottle. "What's up?"

"Well, I was wondering," I said. "Uh . . ."

Kiki drummed her fingers impatiently. "Uh, what? I don't want my fish sticks to get cold."

"Has anyone said anything to you about me?"

Her eyes narrowed. "What do you mean?"

"I don't know, like, have you heard anything like, I might not be who I say I am?"

"You mean like the other day, with the spy stuff? I think half the people believed you, and half thought you were being ridiculous. Although that thing you did to Ross seemed, like, straight out of the Avengers or something. But I haven't heard anything besides that."

"Okay, thanks."

We walked back to the table. If a kid had been spreading rumors about me, Kiki definitely would have known.

That meant it was an adult.

😢 😎 😃

After lunch, I went to the nurse's office, where Nurse Raposo was drinking tea and reading a magazine.

"Somebody knows," I told her.

She looked up. "Somebody knows what?"

"Who I really am." I sat down on one of the nap-and-feel-better tables. "They might not know for sure, but they have a hunch. Someone went to the police about a strange boy in town, and the police went to the Kinders' house."

"I can't believe it," she said. "Well, don't pay attention to them. No one can do anything without proof, and no one can get proof with a search warrant, and no one can get a search warrant without probable cause."

I stared at her, totally confused.

"I watch a lot of police shows on TV," she explained. "So. Did you bring me your list of dos and don'ts?"

"I didn't," I said. "I got really busy. I will."

"Are you planning on going to Field Day on Sunday?" asked the nurse. "You have to be very careful, you know. Don't try to do too much."

"Oh, you don't have to worry about me, I promise."

I didn't tell her the real reason she didn't have to worry.

Which was that I'd be gone by then.

The next day was Friday. It was going to be my last day in school, although I was the only one who knew that, of course. So I decided to have a little fun. Well, my version of fun, anyway.

The first thing I did was start raising my hand again, every time Mrs. Huggle asked a question. It was incredibly obnoxious, I admit it, but I couldn't help myself. I wanted them to remember me as the smartest human they'd ever known.

"Perhaps you'd like to give someone else a chance, Arnold?" asked Mrs. Huggle, staring at my outstretched hand after she'd asked the class a fairly easy math question.

"Sure thing," I said. "Ross, why don't you give this one a try?"

Ross, who'd been using his book as a pillow, lifted his head upright with a snap. "What? Huh? Did somebody say something?"

"What's the square root of eighty-one, Ross?" I asked him. "Mrs. Huggle would like to know. Or, Brett, maybe you know the answer?"

Ross rubbed his eyes and then closed them, as if he were trying to wake himself from a nightmare, but when he opened them again, we were all still there. Brett tried to disappear into his chair.

"The square root of what?" asked Ross.

"Eighty-one," I repeated. "I'll give you a hint. It's less than ten and more than eight."

"Uh, nine?" guessed Brett.

I clapped heartily. "Nailed it!"

Brett looked like he wanted to grind me up into zombie stew. The rest of the class was giggling in shocked glee, but Mrs. Huggle was not amused. "Okay, Arnold, that's enough."

"Sorry, Mrs. Huggle."

I glanced over at Sarah Anne. She was staring straight ahead, but I think there was a small smile at the corners of her mouth.

Later, at lunch, I went all the way on the spy story.

"So I heard from my parents," I told everyone at my table, and the three nearest tables, too. "There's a possibility I may have to join them on their mission. It's top secret, so I can't say a lot about it, but if I do go and never come back, please don't try to contact me—it could be dangerous."

"This is a joke, right?" Evan said. "Tell me you're kidding."

"Nope, not a joke, "I said. "Why do you think I pulled that move on Ross? I was practicing. But don't worry. If I have to go, I'm definitely not leaving before your party."

Kiki narrowed her eyes at me. "Why do I get the feeling there's something you're not telling us?"

"There's A LOT I'm not telling you." I took a handful of jelly beans and stuffed them in my mouth. "But it's for your own safety. If you knew certain things, than you might be in harm's way."

That part was true, anyway.

"Fine, be that way." Kiki grabbed her tray and stood up. "I'm not hungry anymore." She didn't even look at me as she walked away.

I wanted to shout after her, "I'll tell you everything just as soon as I can!"—but I didn't, of course. I just sat there at the table, answering silly questions about my parents' lives as secret agents. But it was okay, I could handle it.

After all, it was going to be my last lunch table ever.

LET'S PARTY!

Finally it was Saturday night—the night of the party! As we pulled into Evan's driveway, Jenny put her hand on my arm.

"Now, Arnold," she said, "I want to be sure you realize you don't have to do this if you don't want to. Jumping into a sleepover is a big step, especially since you're just getting used to being around human children. Are you sure you can handle it?"

"I'll be okay," I said. "Evan only invited two of us, and Kiki can't stay for the sleepover part because she's a girl. If I don't stay, Evan won't have any friends with him on his birthday."

Jenny smiled. "You're a good boy, Arnold," she said.

"I'm not a boy," I reminded her.

"Details, details," she said. "Go on now." But before I got out of the car, I looked at her.

"I just want to thank you for everything you've done for me. You've been so nice, and I really appreciate it."

She frowned. "You're welcome, but where'd that come from?"

"I'm not sure," I said. "I guess I just wanted to say it."

"Go have fun." She waved me out of the car. "See you tomorrow."

I got out of the car and walked up to Evan's front door without looking back.

There was a giant sign hanging over the front door:

HAPPY BIRTHDAY, EVAN!

I rang the doorbell. Evan's mom answered the door and gave me a much friendlier smile than the last time I saw her.

"Hello again, Arnold!"

"Hello again, Evan's mom."

She howled in laughter. "Ha-ha-ha-ha-ha-ha! You can call me Mrs. Brantley."

"Okay. Hi, Mrs. Brantley."

"Come in, please! Evan is just getting dressed."

"Getting dressed?" I asked. "Hasn't he been dressed all day?"

Mrs. Brantley guffawed again. "You are hilarious, Arnold! Well, Evan wanted to look especially nice for the big party tonight."

I wasn't sure that two guests qualified as a big party, but I decided not to say that out loud.

"Is Kiki here?" I asked Mrs. Brantley.

"Not yet, but she should be arriving any minute."

"Where are your dogs?"

"Oh!" She laughed. "I know they made you uncomfortable, so they're at my sister's house for the night."

"You didn't have to do that," I told her, but she wasn't really listening. She led me into their TV room, which had a ton of games set up all around, plus a big machine that said MAKE YOUR OWN COTTON CANDY on the side. Mrs. Brantley pointed at the machine. "Would you like some? It's just as good as at the circus!"

"Oh, no thank you," I said, already wondering how I was going to avoid all the food that was going to be offered. "I actually ate before I came over."

"Who eats before they go to a birthday party?" Mrs. Brantley sat down on the couch and motioned for me to sit, too. "Evan said you were an interesting fellow, and he was right. Where did you say you moved from again?"

"Actually, I didn't say," I told her.

"Oh, right!" Mrs. Brantley said, extremely cheerfully. "Well then, where *are* you from?"

"I grew up all over the place. My family moved a lot."

"And where are your parents now?"

"Overseas."

"I see." The doorbell rang, much to my relief. Mrs. Brantley jumped up. "Well, that must be our other guest!"

She ran to the front door and greeted Kiki with the same over-enthusiasm she had given me. Kiki skipped into the TV room and immediately raided the cotton candy machine.

"So I have one taker!" said Mrs. Brantley. She glanced up the staircase. "I'll go see what's keeping Evan."

"Hmmmph," Kiki mumbled to me, through a mouth full of cotton candy. "When did you get here?"

"A few minutes ago," I said. "Evan's mom is sure acting a little strange today. She's being super friendly."

Kiki laughed. "Have you met Evan? That weirdness had to come from somewhere."

"I haven't asked you yet," I said, "but how did you two become friends? You seem so . . . different."

Kiki chomped thoughtfully on her cotton candy. "Evan and I met in nursery school," she said. "All the other kids were playing with dolls and dinosaurs, and the two of us just wanted to eat glue." She paused. "Then he got sick and disappeared for a while, and according to my parents, I asked them every night where he was. When he came back, his leg was gone, and everyone else in school was scared of him. But

I knew he was the same old Evan, who just wanted to eat glue. And even though we don't have that much in common anymore, we've been friends ever since."

"We sure have!" said a voice behind us. Kiki and I turned around and there was Evan. He was wearing a shirt that said BIRTHDAY BOY! but the *boy* was crossed out and replaced by *man*.

Kiki and I ran up to him. "Birthday man!" we hollered. "Happy birthday!"

Evan seemed so happy to see us, and I was immediately glad I had made the decision not to leave until tomorrow.

"I have a ton of fun things planned for us!" Evan announced. "First we're going to play some games, then we're going to go jump on the trampoline, and then we're going to have cheeseburgers and chocolate pie, and then we're going to go upstairs and watch a scary movie before we go to sleep."

"Sounds amazing!" Kiki said. "I love all those things!"

"Me, too," I chimed in, even though I don't play games, I can't jump, I definitely shouldn't eat cheeseburgers or chocolate pie, and I've never been asleep.

And watching a scary movie doesn't really sound all that great either, to tell you the truth.

But guess what?

It ended up being SO MUCH FUN.

First of all, jumping is easy when you're on a trampoline.
It does all the work for you!

"I'm going so high!" I said to Evan and Kiki, as we bounced
up and down. "This is amazing!" I was so excited that I yelled,
"Watch this!" and lifted my two legs over my head in midair
(zombies can't run very well, but our arms and legs are
super elastic).

Evan and Kiki stared at me in shock. "Where'd you learn
to do that?" Evan asked.

Whoops. I immediately put my legs down. "Uh . . . I've taken a lot of gymnastics classes."

"That's not gymnastics," Kiki said. "That's freaky-deaky-astics." Then she held her arms over her head. "But I'll have you know, you're looking at the world champion trampoliner. Check this out!"

She started doing flips, handstands, and cartwheels. Evan looked at her like she was crazy—and also like she was the luckiest person in the world to have two legs so she could do all that crazy stuff.

"Whoa!" she cried, as she landed on her butt after a particularly wild flip.

"Be careful!" I said. "You could hurt yourself!"

She laughed. "It's worth the risk!"

We all kept jumping, almost touching the sky. Looking at the happiness on Evan's face, I understood the importance of friendship and having people you could count on, and trust, and have fun with.

And that was when I felt it. All of a sudden, I couldn't bear the thought of leaving Evan and Kiki. My first friends ever.

I know it sounds crazy, but I started to wonder if maybe I didn't have to run away after all. Maybe there was a way I could find my old home but still keep my new friends.

Maybe they were worth the risk.

zomBIE ATTACK!

After the trampoline, and the games (I tried to pin the tail on the donkey and ended up pinning it on the couch), and the chocolate pie (I ate the jelly beans on the icing), we settled in to watch the scary movie.

"It's called ZOMBIE ATTACK!" Evan said.

Oh, great.

😵 🧁 😄

The movie was about—you guessed it—a zombie attack. It took place in a small town, and the main part of the story was about a family who had just moved there, and the mom was the town doctor, and the daughter was infected with a virus that turned her into a bloodthirsty, human-hunting zombie, and she led an attack on the town, and so the mom had to decide whether or not to destroy her own daughter.

During a slow part of the movie, Kiki punched me in the shoulder. "Hey, Arnold, I don't know why I never thought about this before," she said. "But if you put your middle initial together with your last name, it spells zombie."

"But it's spelled differently," Evan pointed out. "Z-O-M-B-E-E."

Kiki rolled her eyes. "Yeah, duh, I got that."

"People have been making fun of me about that for years," I said, trying to sound as natural as possible. "Maybe I should change my last name to Frankenstein."

Evan cracked up. "Good thing you're about as opposite to a zombie as anyone could ever be!"

"What do you mean?" I asked him.

"Well, zombies are horrible monsters who eat people's brains. You're, like, the nicest, quietest, most polite kid I've ever met."

"Zombies don't actually exist," Kiki said, as if she were talking to a couple of three-year-olds. "Everybody knows that."

"My dad says you can never be too sure," Evan said.

"Your dad?" I said. Then I realized his dad hadn't come home yet. "Where is your dad, anyway? Is he still at work?"

But before he could answer, the doorbell rang.

"Noooooooo!" said Kiki. Then she ducked under a blanket. "If that's my mom, tell her I'm not here. Tell her a zombie ate my brain!"

"That's not funny," I said.

Kiki looked hurt for a second, then recovered and punched my shoulder. "Gosh, it's just a movie. Lighten up."

It did turn out to be Kiki's mother, coming to get her.

"But, Mom!" Kiki wailed. "I need to watch the rest of the movie!"

Kiki's mom laughed. "Not tonight you don't, honey. It's getting late, these boys need to be heading to bed."

Kiki whined and moaned for a few more minutes, but finally she pulled herself up off the couch and put her shoes and socks back on.

"That was so fun, Evan," she said, giving him a big hug. "Thank you for having me, and happy birthday."

"You're welcome, and thanks," Evan said, beaming.

Then Kiki turned to me and gave me a big hug, too. For a minute I thought she was going to break my bones. It was scary. And nice.

"Wow, you're strong," I said.

"You're darn right I am," she said, releasing me. "Take care of the birthday man, and I'll see you in school on Monday."

"I'll be there," I said.

Part of me meant it.

A LATE NIGHT SURPRISE

Finally it was time for bed. The movie ended with all the humans living happily ever after, and all the zombies destroyed, as usual.

"Zombie movies are so silly," I told Evan, as we brushed our teeth. "I mean, Kiki is right, they don't even exist."

"How do you know?" he said. "Maybe they do exist, but we're protected from them, because if they lived near us, they really would want to eat our brains. You never know."

"I *do* know," I said.

He looked at me with a funny expression on his face. "Are you just saying that because your middle initial and your last name together spell Zombee?"

"No, of course not," I added quickly. "Now that I think about it, I agree with you. You can't be too careful."

Sometimes it's better to be agreeable than to be right.

We put on our pajamas and went into his room, where he had a bunk bed. I took my contact lenses out right before we turned out the light.

"I'll sleep on the top," I said.

"Are you sure? You're not scared of falling out or anything?"

"Nope."

The only thing I was scared of was Evan seeing the red streak across my eyes.

We'd been laying in bed for about ten minutes, talking about silly stuff, when we heard the front door open downstairs.

"Evan?" a man's voice called. "Birthday man, are you still up?"

"Dad!" Evan hollered. "Yay!" He sprang out of bed. "Come meet my dad! He works crazy hours, sometimes all night, but he promised he'd come back before we fell asleep to wish me a happy birthday. And he did!"

Evan raced out of the room and sprinted down the stairs. I climbed down the bunk bed ladder, quickly went to the bathroom to put in a new pair of lenses, and then headed downstairs.

Evan was bear-hugging his dad, so I couldn't see his dad's face. A brand-new bicycle with a bow on it was leaning up against the wall.

"You got me a bike!" Evan exclaimed. "I can't believe it!"

"Ten-speeder," said Evan's dad. "That's a real man's bike right there."

"Wow! Thanks!"

Evan's dad looked up and noticed me. He smiled. "And who's this?"

"Oh, right!" Evan said, excited to introduce us. "This is Arnold. He's new in school, but he's already one of my best friends. Kiki had to go home because she's a girl, but Arnold is sleeping over."

"Well, hey there, Arnold." He walked over to shake my hand. "I'm Horace Brantley. My wife told me she met you a few days back, for a brief minute. I'm very glad to welcome Evan's new friend to our house."

We shook hands. He was tall, with a friendly but stern look in his eyes. He had some sort of military hat on, and a red beard that was already turning gray. He seemed familiar, but I couldn't figure out why.

He looked at me for a long time. "New in school, eh, Arnold? And why is that? Your family just move here?"

"Well, not exactly," I said. "I'm just staying with my

aunt and uncle for a while while my parents are away on assignment."

Mr. Brantley chuckled. "Away on assignment? That sounds intriguing. What kind of assignment?"

"I'm not really supposed to say," I said.

"They're some sort of spies or secret agents," Evan chimed in.

"Ah, I see." Mr. Brantley bent down, and I thought I saw a flicker of something in his eyes, like he just remembered something. "What's your last name, Arnold?"

"Ombee," I told him. "O-M-B-E-E."

"Rhymes with zombie, huh? Look out, Evan, he might bite us and then we'll be zombies, too!" He roared with laughter, then stood up and took his jacket off. "You two go on back to bed, now. I've got to go get some supper and talk with Mom."

"But, Dad!" Evan moaned. "You just got home."

"I know, son, but it was a busy day today, and I have to eat. Defending our nation can really work up a guy's appetite."

Evan looked at me. "My dad's the regional commander of the National Martial Services. How cool is that?"

"Very cool," I said, but a sharp chill ran up my spine.

Mr. Brantley gave his son one last hug. "Hope you had a great birthday," he said to Evan, but he was looking at me.

"Thanks, Dad," Evan said.

As we headed back up the stairs, Evan was talking a mile a minute. "I can't believe my dad got me a bike. That's so awesome. I already have a bike, but it's old. Do you have a bike?"

He kept talking, but I wasn't listening anymore. My mind was racing a mile a minute with other thoughts. Thoughts of fear, and panic, and survival.

Because I knew who Evan's dad was.

THE SHADOW

I crawled up to the top bunk, with one thought running through my head.

I recognized him. But maybe he didn't recognize me.

"Arnold? Are you asleep?"

"Not yet."

Not ever.

Evan sighed deeply and happily. "This was the best birthday. I'm really glad you're here."

"I'm really glad I'm here, too." Which had been totally true, until about four minutes ago.

"I remember when I got the bunk beds," Evan said, sleepily. "I begged my parents for a long time to get them. They kept saying no, they were too dangerous. But finally I talked them into it. I wanted them for sleepovers. I was going to have a lot of sleepovers with the bunk beds."

"Cool."

"But I didn't," Evan said. "You ended up being my first sleepover."

I whistled. "Wow. I'm honored."

"Ha! You should be." And then, two seconds later, he was asleep.

I lay there for a few minutes, listening to the rhythm of Evan's breathing. I thought about how confusing the last few days had been. How I'd made up my mind to leave, but then I changed my mind and wasn't sure, and how seeing Evan's dad reminded me of the danger I would be putting everyone in—including myself—if I really did stay.

At least I had all night to think about it.

I was staring out the window, looking at the stars in the night sky and thinking about how fun it had been to jump on the trampoline with Evan and Kiki, when I heard the bedroom door creak open.

A sliver of light from the hallway streaked in, just enough for me to see the shadow of a person standing in the doorway.

"Hello?" I said.

The shadow didn't answer.

Evan kept snoring.

"Who is that?" I asked, my voice trembling just a little bit.

"Why aren't you asleep, Arnold?" the shadow whispered. "Not tired?"

"Mrs. Brantley? Is that you?" I was pretty sure it wasn't, but I asked anyway.

"Nope. Try again." The shadow moved closer, and I saw that it was carrying something big. "I have a hunch why you're not tired. It's because you don't get tired. Isn't that right?"

By now, the shadow was standing right by the bed. I heard a click, and a bright flashlight suddenly blinded me.

"You can't fool me, Arnold Z. Ombee," hissed the shadow. "You can't fool me with those fake blue eyes, and that friendly smile, and that new-kid-in-school act. I recognized you the second I saw you." He turned the flashlight up toward his own face, and I saw Mr. Brantley leaning in, with a wild look in his eyes. "Just like I know you recognized me." He leaned in closer. "Because we've met before, haven't we, Norbus Clacknozzle?"

"I don't think so," I managed to croak.

"Oh, I'm afraid we have," he said. "But guess what? It wasn't even me who spotted you. My wife knew who you were, the second she saw you. She tipped me off. How's that for some detective work?"

I thought back to the other day, when I met Mrs. Brantley on the walk home. I'd forgotten all about that when I tried to figure out who'd called the authorities.

And I'm supposed to be super smart.

"But I told her, let's not jump to conclusions," said the shadow. "We don't want to accuse an innocent young boy, now, do we? Let's throw Evan a little party, make sure he invites you, and then we'll know for sure." Mr. Brantley held up the big thing he'd brought into the room. With a growing sense of dread I realized what it was.

A bag of salt.

AvoiD salt. Humans Will use salt to Destroy you every chance they Get.

He was going to do a Salt Melt to paralyze me right then and there, while his son slept soundly next to us.

Without even thinking, I grabbed the flashlight out of his hand and shined it in his face to blind him. Then, when he held his hand up to shield his eyes, I whacked him on the head with it.

"OW!" he cried out in pain.

I jumped out of bed, climbed down the ladder, and started running for the door.

Evan stirred. "Hello?" he mumbled. "What's going on? Dad, is that you?"

"Go back to sleep, son," Mr. Brantley said. He grabbed me, trying to stop me from leaving, but I slipped out of his grasp. Then I took the blanket that was covering Evan and threw it over his father's face, but I couldn't escape, because Mr. Brantley was blocking the door. I decided to try to jump out the window, even though we were on the second floor. But by then, he'd gotten rid of the blanket and was running after me.

Mr. Brantley grabbed the salt bag just as I was opening the window, but as he tried to pour it on me, I ducked out of the way. He tried again, and I realized I had no choice. I had to go for it. I had to do it again.

If a human attacks you, immediately employ the zombie zing.

I reached out with my right hand and squeezed his left shoulder. "What the—!" said Mr. Brantley.

And then he couldn't move.

Unable to control his legs, Mr. Brantley started to tip forward toward the window. I ran and opened it. Then, as he fell past me, I pushed him as hard as I could—as hard as I've ever pushed anything in my whole non-life.

"ARRRGGHH!" cried Mr. Brantley, as he disappeared through the window.

Two seconds later, I heard a *thud* as he landed on the front lawn.

"DAD!!!!" cried Evan, who was fully awake by now. "ARNOLD? WHAT'S HAPPENING?"

But I didn't stick around to answer Evan's question.

I flew out of the room as fast as my rubbery legs could take me, headed down the stairs, through the hallway, and out the front door. Then I started running—or doing my

version of running—and I didn't stop for ten whole minutes, until my legs collapsed and I fell down in a heap.

I was sweating yellow goo all over my hands and feet. I wasn't breathing hard—because I don't breathe at all—but I just couldn't run anymore. After a short rest, I got up and started walking. And walking, and walking, and walking.

I had no idea what to do, and I had no idea where to go.

But I knew one thing.

I wasn't going back.

THE WALK

When you're walking along a road at night, and there's no one around, and there no sound except the wind brushing through the trees, and there's nothing to look at except stars and blackness, you think of the strangest things.

You picture what it's like to have a real family, and a mom who loves you.

You imagine what it's like to be a human boy.

You wonder what life would be like if you only had one leg.

You pretend to know what chocolate pie tastes like.

You sing that weird song that Lester plays every morning in the bathroom when he's taking a shower.

People are strange

When you're a stranger.

Faces look ugly

When you're alone.

I kept walking.

It started to rain. Then the rain stopped and water on the road made it slippery. Then it went from dark to semi-dark, and you could kind of see your hand in front of your face, but it looked like a gray blob. Then the darkness faded, and light announced the beginning of a new day.

And the whole time, I walked. I kept walking and walking, until I saw a place I recognized.

Clarendon Hill.

This was where I'd been, just a few weeks ago. Where everything ended, and everything began, and everything changed.

I kept walking.

And then I saw it.

The ditch that I fell into where I hit my head and forgot everything.

But maybe I *didn't* forget everything.

Maybe I never knew *anything*.

My legs suddenly felt very tired, and I found myself walking toward that ditch, as a place to hide from the world while I figured out what to do next, all over again.

I crossed the street toward the ditch, just under the WELCOME TO CLARENDON HILL sign. I leapt down and was immediately greeted with the biggest shock of my young semi-life.

I wasn't alone.

A girl was there.

And she didn't seem all that shocked to see me.

THE POEM

It was still a little dark, but I could make her out well enough. The first thing I recognized was the pink ribbon in her hair. She was laying with her back against the side of the ditch, with a small red bag next to her.

"Oh, hey," I said.

She said nothing.

"It's me, Arnold. From school."

She didn't seem scared at all, or even surprised that someone else had just jumped into the ditch where she was hiding. (I mean, I *think* she was hiding. What else does one do in a ditch?) She wouldn't look at me, but she did move over a little bit, so I could sit down. She was very still and seemed very calm.

Maybe she was actually glad to see me, because that meant she wasn't alone anymore.

We sat there for about twenty minutes, just staring into space. I didn't know what to say to her. Finally I had an idea.

"I'm sorry, I forget your name," I said, which wasn't true. "What is it again?"

The girl stared up at the sky.

"Sally Anne?"

She shook her head no, quickly, back and forth.

"Sheila Mae?"

More head shakes.

"Carrie Jane?"

She let out a frustrated grunt, then reached into her red bag and pulled out her spelling board. She held it out, like she wanted me to hold it for her, so I did. She started pointing at letters with her right hand, but she was going so fast I couldn't keep up.

"Slower!" I said. "Please!"

An annoyed expression crossed her face, but she made a wiping motion across the board, then started again. This time I could keep up as her fingers brushed against each letter. S-A-R-A-H A-N-N-E.

"Sarah Anne. That's right!"

A tiny smiled crossed her lips, then quickly disappeared.

"Nice to see you again. I'm Arnold."

She wrote on her board: I REMEMBER. THE PUDDING EATER.

"Actually," I said, "can I tell you a secret? I'm not Arnold. I'm Norbus." I paused. "It's a long story."

She wrote: I BET.

"Why are you here?" I asked her.

She shook her head like she didn't want to answer.

"I was in this ditch once before," I said. "Actually, I fell in and hit my head. And then I woke up and just hid in here because I was scared."

No response.

"I hid here all night," I went on. "I was alone. I didn't know where I'd come from, and I had no place to go. But I knew I couldn't stay here because the same people who were after me would come back. So I ran. I ran, and I ran, and I ran until I couldn't run anymore. And that's when two people found me and took care of me." I noticed she was looking at me for the first time. Not at my shoulder, but staring intensely into my eyes. "And since then," I went on, "I've met other people who also want to take care of me, or be my friend. And I realized that no matter how bad things are, or how scary the world is, there is always someone who will help you. A lot of someones, actually."

The sun peeked out from the horizon.

"Are you running away? Is that why you're here?"

She shrugged, then motioned for me to pick up the board. Her right hand started moving.

I COME HERE SOMETIMES. BUT NEVER BEFORE AT NIGHT.

"Does it have to do with something that happened in school? You can tell me. I won't tell anyone, I promise."

I LOST MY HORSE.

"I'm really sorry," I said.

I AM ALL ALONE.

"Want to hear something funny?" I asked her. "I thought you were lucky, because people didn't bother you."

THEY WERE IGNORING ME. IT'S EASIER THAT WAY.

"For you or for them?"

FOR THEM. AND I GUESS MAYBE FOR ME, TOO.

"Oh," I said. "I guess it gets lonely sometimes, huh?"

YES.

I didn't know what to say to that, except the truth. "I will be your friend, Sarah Anne, and you won't have to be alone."

SOMETIMES I SCREAM, BUT NO ONE CAN HEAR ME. NOT EVEN MY PARENTS.

"That's like me," I told her. "When I try to yell, nothing comes out."

She stared, just past my eyes.

"I think we all feel that way sometimes," I said.

We sat quietly for a while, until I noticed that her left hand was balled up into a fist, and there was something inside it. It looked like a crumpled-up piece of paper.

I pointed. "What's that?"

She slowly opened her hand and lifted it up to me. Before I read it, I knew what it was.

"Is it a poem? Can I read it?"

She handed it to me. It was called "Hope."

I read it out loud.

In darkness it is hard to see what's in front of you
Shapes are blurred and there's nothing to hold on to
So I wait for the light and search for the brightest spot
Even if some are against you, most are not.

I looked at Sarah Anne. "Wow, that's beautiful." She was staring just past me, as usual. Her board was still in her hand, but she didn't say anything.

I held Sarah Anne's poem up to the sky, where the sun was just rising. "I don't think we should stay here anymore.

I think we should go back to school and see if this is really true. Everyone is probably just starting to gather for Field Day, and we should go. Okay?"

She waited for about a minute before answering.

OKAY.

And we began the long walk back, to the people who were against us, and the people who were not.

THE RETuRN

When Sarah Anne and I walked up to the school, I noticed two things right away.

The first was a big sign taped to a fence near the jungle gym.

FIELD DAY TODAY! COME ONE, COME ALL!

The second was that there were police cars all over the place.

We had reached the edge of the softball field when I first saw the police cars, and I froze. Bill and Jenny were standing by the front doors, talking to Mrs. Huggle.

I started walking away.

"I don't want to see them," I said to Sarah Anne. "They will be so angry with me. They won't understand."

She tugged my arm until I stopped walking. Then she tugged my arm again and turned me around.

The next thing I knew, three people started rushing toward us. I didn't recognize them, and I immediately got scared again. But it wasn't me they were looking for, it was Sarah Anne. Two adults, who were probably her parents, were the first to reach us.

"Sarah Anne, honey!" cried the woman. "Where have you been? You scared us half to death!"

"Almost all the way to death!" said the man. "We were petrified!"

They grabbed her and hugged her so hard, I was surprised that she didn't cry out in pain. The third person was a boy, who looked a little younger than her. As he waited for his parents to finish hugging Sarah Anne, he turned to me. "Do you know my sister?"

"A little."

"Did you rescue her?"

"Absolutely not," I told him. "Actually, I think it's the other way around."

Sarah Anne's parents released her, and the boy looked up at his sister.

"Don't leave again," he said.

She took out the board and handed it to her mother, who held it as Sarah Anne wrote.

I WON'T.

I suddenly heard a yell: "THERE HE IS! DON'T LET HIM GET AWAY!"

Mr. Brantley had spotted me.

Everyone started running in our direction. There must have been at least ten policeman, ten soldiers who were dressed like Mr. Brantley, plus a bunch of teachers, parents, and students. And Bill and Jenny. And Lester. And Kiki. And Evan.

Mr. Brantley reached me first. He had an angry look on his face and a big sling on his arm. For a few seconds, I was actually relieved he was okay. He was Evan's dad, after all—even if he did want to give me the Salt Melt.

"Surprised to see me?" he said coldly.

"I—I wasn't sure. I thought . . . maybe you were hurt. Or still paralyzed."

"Takes more than a Zombie Zing and a broken arm to keep me down," he said. "They designed those things to only last a few minutes anyway. Just long enough to scare the heck out of people, without actually hurting them."

I stared at him in shock. "How—how do you know what a Zombie Zing is?"

"It's my job to know." Then he grabbed my arm, and I knew I was in real trouble.

"HE HAS RETURNED!" Mr. Brantley announced to the crowd. "BELIEVE ME WHEN I TELL YOU—THIS THING IS NOT HUMAN. THIS THING IS NOT A BOY. THIS IS A DANGEROUS CREATURE!" He looked at me and shook my arm hard. "Tell them who you really are," he sneered.

I kept my head down. I couldn't bear to look at anyone, especially the Kinders. "My name is Norbus Clacknozzle," I said. "I am . . . a zombie."

The crowd gasped.

"SEE, I TOLD YOU!" yelled Mr. Brantley. Then he looked at me and snorted. "You must have known you couldn't have gotten away with this forever." I didn't have time to answer him, though, because as soon as Bill and Jenny reached us, they made a protective circle around me.

"Stay back!" Bill shouted. "You have no right to hurt this boy! He is young and innocent, just like all the other children at this school!"

"Make one move and you'll be arrested for treason!" Mr. Brantley said. "I'll see to it myself!"

"Then so be it. But before you take me away, I need to tell these people what's really happening here." Jenny held her hand up to hush the still-buzzing crowd. "A few years

ago, the government set up a top secret division of the military, which they labeled Project Z. It was a laboratory built deep in the heart of the Arizona mountains, called the Territory, where a group of top scientists gathered to regenerate a series of afterlife humans." She paused for a moment in front of the silent crowd. "In other words, zombies."

"This is nonsense," sputtered Mr. Brantley, but someone in the crowd said "Quiet!" and someone else yelled "Let her speak!" Mr. Brantley's face turned red, but he fell silent.

"Go on, Jenny," said Bill, quietly.

"The goal of the project," said Jenny, "was to create a population of zombies similar to those created in popular culture, such as movies and television, and then unleash them onto an unsuspecting public. This would cause panic, and the public would then turn aggressive toward these outsiders. The government thought it would be a much-needed boost for national morale if we were to suddenly confront a common outside enemy, and mercilessly defeat it." Jenny glanced at Bill, who nodded at her to keep going. "The zombies were going to be released into the general population within the next year, and of course would have been systematically, and eventually completely, wiped out. But a few weeks ago, several of them escaped. All were quickly caught and returned to the Territory, except one. And you know what? That single, escaped zombie ruined everything." Jenny paused and put her hand on my shoulder. "Because he turned out to not be scary at all. He turned out to be a wonderful little boy."

All eyes turned to me, as people tried to absorb this shocking information.

"That's the craziest story I've ever heard!" shouted someone in the crowd.

"Ridiculous!" yelled another.

Mr. Brantley held up his hand, and the crowd went quiet. "As regional commander of the National Martial Service, I can assure you all that this story is absurd, right out of a science fiction movie. There is no such project!"

"There is," Jenny said, quietly. "I know this for a fact."

"HOW?" said Mr. Brantley, raising his voice. "How could you possibly know this?"

There was a pause, as Jenny gathered the strength and courage for what she was going to say next.

"Because I was the lead scientist on the project," she said.

I stared at her. "You were?"

She nodded. "Yes, I was. My firm, J. K. Labs, developed the technology and the software." Then she took my cold face in her warm hands.

"I made you," she said.

The crowd gasped, then fell silent. The only thing you could hear was a plane buzzing faintly in the sky.

"The identities of the scientist team members were kept so top secret that no one knew who we were." She looked at Mr. Brantley. "Not even the regional commander of the National Martial Service."

Mr. Brantley's face went white as he realized that Jenny was telling the truth—she had run the secret lab.

Bill looked at me. "We couldn't tell you," he said. "It was too dangerous. But yes, Jenny worked there until a year ago, when she realized exactly what the secret project was for. First, she decided she didn't want to be a part of it. And then, she decided she'd try to do whatever she could to stop it."

Evan and Kiki both stared at me in shock.

"Is it true?" sputtered Kiki.

"Are you really . . . a zombie?" Evan asked.

I stared at the ground. "Yes."

"And your fake name is Arnold Z. Ombee?" Kiki asked. "That's the best you could come up with?"

I didn't look up, but I nodded. "I didn't want to give up who I really am."

Evan shook his head over and over. "Well, it's such a dumb fake name for an undercover zombie, it's actually perfect."

"I guess it's not," I said. "Look around you. Everyone here knows who I am now, don't they?"

"Well, yeah," Evan said.

"With all due respect," Mr. Brantley said, "that's a touching story, and you're a very courageous woman. But regardless, we're not talking about a human boy here. We're talking about a zombie. And zombies do not belong in the general population, no matter how friendly they might be."

"That's right!" hollered a voice from the crowd. "You don't belong here! Go back to where you came from!"

A bunch of kids cheered. And some parents, too.

"QUIET!" Bill roared. "He will stay here with us! We are his family now! We are taking care of him!"

Suddenly there was screaming coming from all directions, as people crowded around us. They were saying all kinds of things.

"Zombies don't have families!"

"The government knows what's best!"

"Show some compassion!"

"You're breaking the law!"

"Leave him alone!"

I looked at the Kinders and saw fear in their eyes. We started backing up, but there was nowhere to run.

"You see?" Lester shouted. "I knew this would happen! I knew it! You guys always want to do what you think is right, but you don't think about the consequences!"

Nurse Raposo and Mrs. Huggle came running over to us. "We can help," Nurse Raposo said. "My car is right over here. We can make a run for it and drive you home before anything else happens."

"And then what?" Jenny said. "Run away? Move to another state? Another country? Or should we just let them take him away, banish him to some government installation where we'll never see him again? No. We'll stay right here."

"Let them arrest us right here at this school, if they have to," Bill added. "We won't back down, and we won't run." He turned to Lester. "And, son, I understand how you feel, I really do. But we're not doing what we *think* is right. We're doing what we *know* is right."

By now, the crowd was closing in, and Mr. Brantley was still holding me tight.

"Stop it!" Kiki screamed. "Everyone, stop! This is crazy! Leave him alone!" But no one was listening to her.

"It's okay," I told her. "Thanks for trying. It's okay." I turned to Evan, who looked like he was about to cry.

"If you hadn't come to my sleepover, none of this would have happened," he said. "I'm sorry. I'm so, so sorry."

"Don't be," I said. "I'm not mad at you. You're my friend." And I flicked him on the neck to prove it. He tried to laugh and flicked me back.

"The Flicker," I said.

"Ghostie," he said.

And right then, his father pinned my arms behind my back. "IT'S OVER," Mr. Brantley announced. "Everyone step back, please. This time, it's really, truly over. You're coming with me so we can sort this out."

I knew what *sort this out* meant. He didn't want to give me the Salt Melt before the whole school. He was going to do it somewhere else. Then he was going to have me shipped back to the Territory.

"Good-bye," I said to the Kinders. "Thank you for being so nice to me."

I closed my eyes, waiting for Mr. Brantley to take me away. I was ready for whatever was going to happen. I was ready to return to whatever I'd been, whoever I'd been, before I began this crazy, in-between existence.

And then, a deafening yell pierced the air.

The arguing and hollering and crying and commotion stopped. Everyone looked around to see where the sound was coming from.

There was another piercing yell. Mr. Brantley let go of me.

People started moving away, making a path for someone to walk through. I couldn't tell who it was at first, and then I saw her.

Sarah Anne. Holding her head up high. And looking straight at me.

This time, when she screamed, people heard her.

☹ 😎 😃

Sarah Anne came up next to me, then stopped. Standing with her were her parents and Ms. Frawley, her aide. Sarah Anne held her right hand out. Ms. Frawley took out the letter board and held it up.

Everyone was silent as Sarah Anne's fingers began to fly.

ARNO

She stopped suddenly and made an erasing motion on the board. Then she started again.

HOW DO YOU SPELL YOUR REAL FIRST NAME?

"N-o-r-b-u-s," I said.

She nodded her thanks and started again.

NORBUS IS MY FRIEND.

She took a deep breath, then continued.

PLEASE DON'T HURT HIM.

Then she put her hand down, walked over to me, and held my hand.

Everyone was completely still and silent. A confused look crossed Mr. Brantley's face as he glanced around. "Whose child is this?" he called out. "Please come claim her."

Sarah Anne's mother stepped up. "This is my child," she said. "And she's never had a friend in her whole life. Please don't take him away from her."

"I know this is hard," Mr. Brantley said, trying to sound calm. "But it's not my decision. This is government policy. This is the law. He needs to go back." His hand clamped back down on my arm, as he began to walk me toward his car. People on both sides of the argument were yelling, but we just kept walking. We were about two steps from the car when one last voice was heard.

"If you take him away from me," the voice said, "I don't know what I'll do."

This time Mr. Brantley stopped.

Because the voice belonged to his son.

Evan stepped forward and stood right next to me. He looked up at his father.

"Arnold is my friend, Dad," Evan said. "I used to be scared of zombies, like everyone else. But now that I know one, I realize that there's nothing to be afraid of. He's kind, and friendly, and not that different from us. I mean, at first I thought he was just another funny-looking kid." He looked at me and smiled. I tried to smile back. "I met Arnold on the bus, and I annoyed him by flicking him in the back of his neck. But then he sat next to me in school, and we became friends. He stuck up for me in front of the other kids. He walked home with me and didn't care about my leg. He eats nothing but jelly beans, and he runs funny, and his skin is almost see-through and he's a genius in school, but other than that he's a lot like the rest of us."

Evan paused for a second. I realized that it had gotten completely silent. Sarah Anne was standing next to her mother, holding her hand, the same way Mr. and Mrs. Kinder had been holding hands when I first met them.

"Don't take my friend away, Dad," said Evan. "It's not fair. It's not fair to me, and it's especially not fair to him."

Mr. Brantley looked down at his son for a long moment. I could feel his grip on my arm loosen.

"Hey!" Kiki added. "Arnold is my friend, too, and a great kid! Everyone likes him." She looked around. "Right, everyone?"

A few kids started nodding their heads. Then, a few more. Then, a few more. I couldn't believe it.

"Arnold—er, Norbus—is my student," Mrs. Huggle said. "One of the smartest I've ever had, in fact. I would like to continue teaching him, if you don't mind."

"He's sweet and kind," said Nurse Raposo. "It's important

for the other children to understand that we are all a lot more similar than we are different. We shouldn't have to fight a common enemy in order to come together as a country."

A bunch of people murmured their approval at that last comment. Then a girl emerged from the crowd, and it took me a minute to realize it was Darlene, Lester's friend. The blue hair was the tip-off.

"Yo," Darlene said. "This cool little guy is pretty much the most fashion-forward dude I've met in my entire LIFE." She walked over to Lester and kissed him on the cheek. "And you kept his secret?" she said to him. "I'm, like, really impressed."

"Yeah, well, you know, like, yeah," Lester said, grinning like . . . well, like someone who's just been kissed by the girl he likes.

"Dad?" Evan said. "What do you say, Dad? Can we protect Arnold? Can we keep him safe here?"

"I . . . I'm just not sure, son," said Mr. Brantley.

It felt like Mr. Brantley was still trying to decide what to do when there was a rustling in the crowd, and I heard voices saying, "Make way!" and "Let me through!" Five seconds later, Ross and Brett emerged from the crowd.

Uh-oh, I thought to myself. *So much for the happy ending.*

They walked over and stood right in front of me. They looked me up and down.

"It's Field Day," Ross said. "Are you gonna play dodgeball with us, or what?"

A cheer went up from the crowd. Mr. Brantley looked down at me, then over at Bill and Jenny Kinder.

Then he let go of my arm.

"I never really got the point of this dang project anyway, to be honest with you," he said. "Fine. I'll take care of it. But nobody can utter a word about this. EVER."

"Understood," said Bill. "Understood."

Mr. Brantley gave me a gentle shove, and I ran over to the Kinders, where they wrapped me up in a giant hug, even giant-er than the last one.

"Thank you, Bill," I said. "Thank you, Jenny."

"Norbus?" Jenny said. "Please call us Mom and Dad."

Meanwhile, Evan was hugging his dad. "You're the best dad ever," he said. "The best." Evan's mom saw me and walked over.

"I had no idea what you'd been through," she said. "Please forgive me."

I shook my head. "You did what you thought was right. There is nothing to forgive."

Lester—who was still smiling from Darlene's kiss—punched me in the shoulder, which kind of hurt a little bit. But it was a good punch.

"Welcome back," he said.

THE CAPTAINS

"It's time for dodgeball, the Field Day Grand Finale!" hollered Coach Hank. "Arnold and Evan, choose up sides! You're captains!"

Evan and I both blinked. "Seriously?" I asked.

"Yes, seriously!" Coach Hank blew the whistle. "I'm never not serious!"

"Coach," Ross said. "His name's actually Norbus."

"Norbus Clacknozzle," Brett said.

They both shook their heads like it was the strangest name they'd ever heard. Which I suppose it was.

"I don't care what his name is!" Coach Hank barked. "As long as he's a winner!"

Evan and I stood in front of the other kids, staring at each other.

"You go first," Evan said.

"Okay." I pointed. "I'll take Joel."

Joel, a tiny red-haired kid who was the quietest kid in

school, stared at me in disbelief. Then he came running over and held his hand out in a fist. I stared up at it.

"Fist bump, dude," he said. "Let's do this."

"Oh, right." I fist-bumped him.

We kept picking until everyone was taken. The game began, and I'd barely picked my ball up when I felt a sharp SMACK! in my ribs.

"NAILED YA!" Ross hollered. "Take a seat, loser!"

I took a seat. I was the first one out on my team, and the whole left side of my body looked like it had been practically caved in by the ball.

It felt great.

FAMILY dINNER

That night at dinner, the four of us held hands and bowed our heads before eating. Not to pray, but to hope—for a world where people are nicer to one another. And nicer to zombies, and animals, and aliens, and any other non-human who doesn't mean them harm.

"Okay, let's eat!" announced Jenny. I mean, Mom.

"Dinner's delicious, old man," said Lester. Bill—I mean, Dad—cooked on Sundays. He only knew how to make one thing—fried chicken—but they all LOVED it.

"Mmmmmm" was the only word anyone said for five minutes.

I looked at them and started wishing. I wished I could eat fried chicken. I wished I could drink orange juice, and jump high without a trampoline, and feel warm. I wished I could sleep.

"What are you thinking about?" Mom asked.

"I don't know," I said. "Just—I wish things could be a little different, I guess. A little easier."

"Wishing things won't make them so," said Dad. "And it's better to be glad for the things you do have than to wish for the things you don't."

I nodded. Parents were really smart, even if they couldn't read *War and Peace* in an hour.

I dug into my jelly beans. They tasted sweeter than usual. I closed my eyes.

"*Now* what are you thinking about?" Lester asked me.

I opened my eyes, looked at each one of them, and smiled.

What *was* I thinking about?

Some are against you, but most are not.

"How happy I am to be home," I said.

April 18, 2027
GT 278
PROJECT Z
THE OUTER BRANCH
ARIZONA

ATTENTION ALL PERSONNEL: General Horace Brantley, regional commander of the National Martial Services, has stepped down from his duties, effective immediately.

General Brantley served with distinction for over twenty years. His most recent responsibilities included heading up PROJECT Z, where he helped manage the breach of security by returning five of the subjects to the Territory within twenty-four hours. He also headed up the search for the one remaining escapee, who continues to elude capture, after a potential sighting last month proved to be a false alarm.

Mr. Brantley will return to the private sector. We wish him well.

PLEASE BE ASSURED: THE SEARCH FOR THE LOST ZOMBIE WILL CONTINUE UNTIL THE SUBJECT IS SECURED.

Micah Garnett
Interim Regional Commander, National Martial Services

ZOMBIE: FRIEND OR FOE?
Final Class Project
By Evan Brantley
Grade 5

INTRODUCTION
Are zombies real?

It's a very good question. I mean, nobody thinks they're real, right? Most people have never even seen or met a zombie. They just know them from movies and TV shows and stuff, where zombies are these weird creatures that come back from the dead and eat human brains and are generally completely scary and disgusting.

But guess what?

That's all made up.

And guess what also?

Zombies ARE real.

It's true! They are. But they're not what you think they are, not even close.

This class project will explore why zombies are so misunderstood and will show that we shouldn't be afraid of certain things just because we don't know very much about them. Because once we do get to know them, we will realize we have a lot more in common than maybe we thought.

Why am I so interested in zombies, you ask?

Well, because as it turns out, I know a zombie.

Personally.

In fact, he's my best friend.

SECTION ONE

Don't believe everything you see or read about zombies.

There are a lot of scary books and movies out there that make zombies out to be horrible, dangerous, flesh-eating monsters.

Nothing could be further from the truth.

In fact, in many ways, zombies are a lot like you and me.

They have two eyes, two ears, two arms, two legs, two feet, two hands, a nose, and a mouth.

They walk and talk. They have hair on their heads. They sneeze.

But in other ways, they are very different.

First of all, they are really, really skinny. Basically they have no fat on their bodies because they don't eat very much.

Also, their skin is almost see-through. Because their hearts don't beat, they don't have blood running through their bodies to provide color and health to the skin.

Another thing about zombie skin is that they freeze when they touch salt. They never talk about that in the scary zombie movies, but it's true. I learned that this year, last month actually, when I also learned about the Salt Melt, which is man's strongest weapon against zombies, because it paralyzes them. I wish we didn't have any weapons against zombies.

Also, they have a red streak that runs across the pupils of both eyes.

And zombies sweat, but it doesn't look like human sweat. It's yellow and sticky, and actually really smelly and gross.

But perhaps the most amazing thing of all is—they don't breathe. That's the one thing that all the movies and TV shows and stuff got right.

Personality-wise, there are many interesting traits to the zombie.

They are super smart. Like, genius level. But they can only think or talk or write in short bursts, because their brains get tired very easily.

They can talk, but they can't yell.

The only thing they eat are jelly beans.

They are scared of animals.

But I think the coolest thing about zombies is that they have their own secret weapon, called the Zombie Zing. The Zombie Zing is a grip that temporarily paralyzes their enemies. It's kind of like the Salt Melt, except it only works if it's a matter of survival. In other words, a zombie can't just use it if he's a little scared of something.

But of all the physical and personality traits that zombies have, maybe the most surprising one of all is this: They are very friendly once you get to know them. And they are not here to hurt us.

It is too bad that humans misunderstand so much about zombies. Maybe one day we can realize that they're not so different from you and me. Except for the not-breathing part.

That part's pretty different, I'll give you that much.

SECTION TWO: JELLY BEANS

There are many theories about why zombies only eat jelly beans.

Some people think it's because jelly beans look like

little brains. I don't think that's the reason, though. And besides, that's totally gross.

Other people think it's because zombies are really skinny so they are always trying to eat a lot of sugar to gain weight. I guess that kind of makes sense, but the only problem is, there are a lot of other things that have a lot of sugar, too, which they don't eat. Like chocolate pie, which is my favorite.

I have my own theory about why zombies eat jelly beans.

Which is, that there *is* no theory.

Because they're zombies. And like animals, they're mysteries, and they do some things that are very different from the way we do things.

I'm sure we're a mystery to them, also. Which is why it would be so much better if we weren't afraid of each other. If we're afraid of something just because it's not like us, then we will never take the time to understand it.

SECTION THREE: WILL THERE COME A TIME WHEN MAN NO LONGER FEARS THE ZOMBIE?

I sure hope so.

There are lots and lots of species in the world. We're all very different, but we all share something very important: the planet and all its resources. Which is why I think we should try to understand and respect each other. I used to be very scared of zombies, but now I know they're just trying to survive, like us.

Zombies were created so that we could wipe them out and become more unified as a nation. I think we would become more unified as a nation if we learned to accept them instead.

But for now, that has to be our secret. Because outside of our small town, no one knows zombies exist.

CONCLUSION

When I found out Norbus Clacknozzle was a zombie, I was really confused and scared. My dad was about to send him back to the Territory, and I would have never seen him again. But I was also scared and confused because I had been taught to be afraid of zombies, to stay away from them, and even to hate them. But then I met one without knowing it, and he became my friend. So I begged my dad to let him stay, and my dad said yes.

That day on the softball field, my teacher, Mrs. Huggle, told me she was really touched by what I said, and that I should turn it into my class project. Which is why I'm writing this now.

Norbus is a zombie, and he is also my best friend. I've learned so much from him, like which jelly beans taste the best, how to pretend to take a nap, and the best way to hide the smell of zombie sweat. (Cheese. Lots and lots of cheese.)

He hasn't shown me how to do the Zombie Zing yet. But that's okay.

Hopefully he'll never need to use it again.

ACKNOWLEdgmENTS

Afterlife humans don't just arrive fully formed. You need a lot of people to create a single zombie.

So I'd love to thank my fellow creators: Anna Bloom, Brianne Johnson, Allie Levick, Nancy Mercado, Dave Bardin, Yaffa Jaskoll, Robin Hoffman, all my pals at Scholastic Book Fairs, and Charlie Greenwald.

Finally, a special shout-out goes to Coco Aysseh, whose bravery and poetic soul are an inspiration to everyone who knows her.

You all deserve a big bag of jelly beans—my treat!

ABOUT THE AUTHOR

© Suzanne Sheridan

TOMMY GREENWALD is the author of many books for children, including the CrimeBiters! series, the Charlie Joe Jackson series, and the football novel *Game Changer*. This is his first book for zombies.

PROJECT Z CONTINUES!

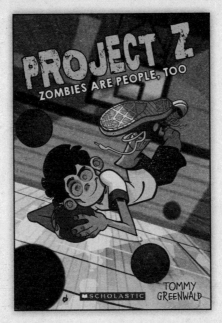

THE ZOMBIE SECRET IS OUT!

Well, sort of. Now scientists at the lab Arnold
escaped from claim they've changed their tune.
Instead of creating zombie enemies, they just want
humans and zombies to be friends.
Too good to be true? Probably!

READ ON FOR A SNEAK PEEK . . .

THE SMARTEST KID IN SCHOOL

There's a phrase that used to run through my head all the time back when I first escaped from the lab.

Humans are the enemy. Humans are dangerous. Humans are the enemy. Humans are dangerous.

Jenny Kinder—who is now, unofficially, my mom—said the scientists at the lab programmed those thoughts into my brain so that I would be aggressive toward people.

She would know, since she was one of the scientists.

Humans are the enemy. Humans are Dangerous.

But guess what? It didn't work. Probably because it's not true.

If they wanted to be accurate, they would have programmed this:

Even though some humans are Dangerous, most aren't. But ALL humans hate homework. Many humans aren't very GooD at math. AnD a

When I entered the fifth grade at Bernard J. Frumpstein Elementary School, most people treated me like a total outsider—probably because I *was* a total outsider. But there were two people who were nice to me: Evan Brantley, who got on my nerves by flicking the back of my neck on my very first bus ride, but quickly became my best pal; and Kiki Ambrose, the most popular kid in the whole school, who decided for some incredibly lucky reason to find me interesting.

At first, all the other kids made fun of me; then, when they saw me temporarily paralyze Ross Klepsaw with the Zombie Zing (it was his fault, I swear), they all got scared of me; and finally, when everyone found out I was a zombie but that I was more interested in being their friend than eating their brains, they accepted me as (almost) one of them.

Which is where the whole tutoring thing comes in.

One day during lunch, a boy named Jimmy Edwards came up to me. I'd barely said five words to him before then, but he slapped me on the back like were old pals.

"Arnold, buddy boy!" he exclaimed. "How goes it?"

I looked up at him. "It goes it pretty well, how goes it with you?"

"Great, great." Jimmy pulled up a chair next to me. "So yeah, Arnold, I got a little problem, to be honest with you."

"What's that?"

"I'm failing English."

"Oh. Gosh, I'm sorry to hear that."

Kiki, who was sitting on one side of me, rolled her eyes. "Get to the point, Jimmy."

"Right." Jimmy glared at Kiki, then turned back to me. "So anyway, Arnold, I was wondering, since you're so smart and everything, maybe you could, like, help me get my grade up?"

I was confused, since the whole process of school had seemed pretty easy to follow so far. "Help you how? If you do the work the class requires, then surely you will succeed."

Jimmy cleared his throat. "Yeah, well, uh, I guess I haven't exactly done the work required."

"Oh. I understand," I said, even though I didn't.

Evan, who was sitting on the other side of me, saw the confusion on my face. "Here's the thing, Arnold. Not all kids are the same. Some kids do their homework, others don't.

Some kids pay attention in class, some kids don't. Some kids like to read, others don't."

"Nobody likes to read," corrected Jimmy.

"That's not true," insisted Evan. "I do, for example."

Jimmy snickered. "No *normal* people."

"Enough, you two," said Kiki. "I love to read, but that doesn't make me any better than kids who don't. We're just different, that's all." She fiddled with the bun in her hair. "The point is, Arnold, that you're like, the smartest kid in the whole school, and Jack needs some help. Will you help him?"

"Of course I will."

That day after school, I taught Jimmy the difference between "its" and "it's," made sure he knew the difference between an adjective and an adverb, and showed him how to use "sluggish" in a sentence. (Eating four ice cream sandwiches at lunch made Timmy sluggish at soccer practice.) Then, for the next week, I helped him with a whole bunch of other stuff.

When Jimmy got an 81 on the test, he ran over to me. "Yo, dude, we did it!"

"You did it," I told him.

"Nah, *we*!" He lifted me up in the air, which wasn't hard

for him to do, since he's very strong and I'm very skinny. "Hey everyone! Arnold here saved my butt! He's like, a genius!"

And that's basically how I became the unofficial tutor for the entire fifth grade class at Bernard J. Frumpstein Elementary School.

"How much are you making for all this tutoring?" Evan asked me one day, while we were jumping on his trampoline.

I did a triple somersault, which is easy for me because my legs are like rubber bands. Extremely pale rubber bands. "Making? What do you mean, making?"

"I mean, how much are you charging for your work?"

"I'm not charging anything," I told him. "I'm doing it because they need my help."

Evan's eyes went wide. "Are you *kidding* me right now? You need be getting paid! Makin' the MOAN-NAY!"

Apparently, there was still a lot I needed to learn about the ways of the humans.

Follow all the cases of the CrimeBiters, and the dog that may or may not be a crime-fighting vampire.